BARBARA ROSE BROOKER

I0541412

SHOULD I SLEEP IN HIS DEAD WIFE'S BED?

Llumina
Press

Requests for permission to make copies of any part of this work should be mailed to Permissions Department, Llumina Press, 7580 NW 5th Street UNIT 16535 Plantation, FL 33318.

ISBN: 978-1-62550-339-8
      978-1-62550-118-9

Printed in the United States of America by Llumina Press

Library of Congress Control Number: 2013920307

DEDICATION

To my daughter Suzy Unger, who makes it possible, and my daughter Bonny Osterman, my angel. Endless love to my son in laws, Henry Unger, Gary Osterman

TABLE OF CONTENTS

Introduction

PART ONE:
LOOKING FOR LOVE

PART TWO:
TRYING TO FIND LOVE, FAME, AND FORTUNE

PART THREE:
CONFLICTS AND CHANGES

PART FOUR:
KATY FINDS IT ALL

INTRODUCTION

I'm sixty-three, and I want to be a movie star. I want everything—fame, fortune, and undying love. I've had it with the ageism in our country. If you don't look like those drippy housewives of Orange County, you're a throwaway. Anyway, my name is Katy Roseman, and I'm a Ph.d psychologist specializing in boomer love. I put my case histories into *Boomer Heat*, a book about the sexual neurosis of aging boomer men, and it's a huge hit. What I'm finding is that these boomer-plus men are terrified of age and want younger women to replace their dead wives: women with money, and no lines, wrinkles, or cellulite. Is love possible in the Viagra generation? The past twenty-two years since my husband dropped dead in Walgreen's, every night I dream that I dance the tango with a tall stranger. I wear a backless black dress, no roll on my back, a slit along the side, black net stockings, tango shoes, and I don't step on his feet. We're madly in love, and it's great, feels like I'm inside a hot rainbow.

No matter how women's roles grow, if she's over sixty, she's considered over-the-hill. Yet, if a boomer-plus man is eighty and has two heads, he's considered a catch.

It kills me.

Part One:

Looking For Love

ON THE PHONE WITH SANDY BERNSTEIN

"*D*o I sleep in their dead wives' beds?" I ask Sandy.

"Honey, tell them to get a new bed. As soon as you sleep with them, you're taking the dead wife's place. The last one I slept with made me have sex in the shower because his wife died in his bed."

"Josh's wife died twenty years ago, and he still won't let me sleep in her bed. I've had it with Josh and his schmootzy ways. He may be a genius, but he's a case. He wears Birkenstocks, has dandruff, has a huge hernia that pops out when he's on top of me, and he's a major hypochondriac and womanizer."

"Dump the schlump!"

"Well, it's research," I reply defensively.

"You've said that for ten years."

"Anyway, I want undying love before I leave the planet. I'm going to date others now. I told Josh. I may even explore sex."

Sandy continues to rant about boomer dating. She's sixty-four and owns a chic menswear shop in San Francisco's Union Square. Over twenty years ago, both re-entry women, we met in a graduate psychology class at San Francisco State University. She's divorced, and her well-known doctor husband left her penniless. She's still paying off debts. After working for years as a fundraiser, she opened her shop and is now doing well.

1

"Anyhoo," she continues in her raspy voice, "I met a seventy-one-year-old real estate tycoon at Monica Bergman's memorial. He lost his wife a year ago and invited me to dinner. He seems really hot. He said his wife fell out of a window."

"Maybe he pushed her."

"Also, he was sniffing and snorting," Sandy sighs. "These boomer-plus guys have allergies, sleep apnea, spray tans, and memory loss. Yet they're in demand. They can have three heads, and women will give them casseroles, tickets to musicals galore, and blow their teeny weenies."

"Tell me about it. Most of my male boomer patients are fixated on age and vaginas."

"Honey, they're all the same. Turn off the lights, blow them, and they'll get off on a horse. The last one I slept with was so quiet I thought he was dead, but he was sleeping."

ROGER BERMAN

"I like a puffed-up vagina. Gloria's is gray and caved in, like a flat tire."

I adjust the pillow behind my back. Roger Berman is my last patient of the day, and he's been talking about this vagina for over thirty minutes. He's been my patient for six months.

"Doc, I really liked Gloria until I saw her vagina. I'm a sensitive guy, as you know, but she lied."

"About her vagina?"

"About her age!" he cries. "She said she was fifty-four, which was a stretch for me, and when I saw her vagina, I knew she's seventy-six, if she's a day."

"A few months ago, you told me how much you liked her—even loved her."

He shrugs his narrow shoulders. "Not my type, but I thought she was interesting and talented. Different from the usual beauties I date. Until this happened. I'm a fair guy, but I don't like lies. I never knew she was seventy-three. Lucky I researched her and got her birth certificate."

"Why does age matter? It has nothing to do with the person."

"It matters. I don't want to spend the rest of my years looking at a caved-in vagina. I want true love."

"True love has nothing to do with vaginas."

He shrugs again. "It does in my book, doc."

"Well, unfortunately, it's time to end our session," I say, brightly.

He sits forward, stretches his neck, and then stands. He's six-foot-three with a trickle of thin, tan, curly hair and pale, tan, empty eyes. He wears designer workout clothes and running shoes.

I stand by the door while he fumbles with the lock, two turns to the right, one to the left. Then he does this double hop thing, smiles, and rushes out of there.

At my desk, I take notes about Roger's vagina obsession. I'm working on a sequel to *Boomer Heat*. I write in Case Histories Two: *Vagina obsession. Lonely. Ego about money and things. In pain. Insecure.*

I draw diagrams of images I've taken from his conversations over the year, trying to find a clue to his obsession.

It's dark now. I turn on the track lights. They make a popping sound. Time to get ready for my date tonight with Josh. I turn off the computer and close the office. For the past ten years, I've been seeing Josh Feldstein, this schmootzy sixty-eight-year-old Nobel Prize winning astronomy professor. He's definitely a commitment phobic, and I'm thinking about ending it.

I live in a huge loft on Mission Street. Once an industrial hat factory, the loft has twenty-foot windows that look out at the San Francisco Bay. Between *Boomer Heat*'s success and my Apple stock, I paid cash for the loft. I painted the entire loft white, and Alberto and Randy, my very good friends, painted the concrete floors pale gray. I turned the guest room downstairs into my office where I see patients. The furnishings are mixed with super contemporary furnishings, flea market wood pieces, and my paintings.

I finish dressing. I'm wearing black skinny jeans, flat boots, and a fitted black jacket. Maybe silver earrings—red lipstick—one more blow to my hair, which hangs below my shoulders. Ten years ago, I met Dr. Josh Feldstein at his lecture on Our Expanding Universe. The Stanford lecture hall was wall-to-wall science groupies. I've always been interested in the universe and the state of the human soul. Anyway, at a wine mixer afterwards, I introduced myself and felt an instant attraction. Shortly after that night, he called, and we've been together ever since, but only on Friday nights.

The doorbell rings.

Professor Josh Feldstein

"Wow, great. That was great," I say, snuggling into his arms. The past hours, we'd made love. Great sex. The kind of sex I'd never had before I met Josh.

In the dark, side-by-side, we hold hands. I watch the rain flood the windows and the lights from the bridge float on the ceiling like candles. Josh's salt and pepper curly hair sticks up like a hat. He's short and stocky, but he hikes regularly and has the body of an athlete. He coughs several times then snorts.

"Allergies," he says.

He pulls the covers over his body, leaving my side of the bed almost empty. Again he's snorting and coughing, and clearing his throat.

"I feel a tickle in my throat, Katy. Please close the windows."

"I need air."

"My allergies. I can't have air."

I get up and close the windows, and shivering, I get into bed and press my body close to his. I whisper, "I bought blueberries for your breakfast. I thought after breakfast we'd go for a walk along the pier. See the ships."

He sighs. Coughs. "I have to leave by seven. I have an important paper to give at the university."

"Uh-huh. You mean *she's* waiting. Your Russian graduate student."

"Helga's a tenant. She helps me with research. I've told you hundreds of times—"

Soon he's snoring. I lie awake, remembering two years ago at his seventieth birthday party at his big Palo Alto house. It was filled with famous astronomers, faculty hotshots, and Josh's female graduate students. I had thought I was there as Josh's exclusive girlfriend, when I noticed him slow dancing to "Okay Hokey Cat" with this twenty-something, slutty-looking Russian girl. She had spiked yellow hair and hostile, pale blue eyes. She wore spiked fuck-me heels and a tank top, and they were dancing like they were fucking. Hello! I got it. No way was I the only one. All those times he had sudden "papers" to give or had to leave early, he was fucking the Russian spy girl. I'd pretended that. So many times, I'd tried to leave him, but then I'd miss him, and one of us would call each other.

"Josh? Are you awake? Josh?"

"I am now," he says sleepily.

"I'm going to date others. I don't want to be a Friday night fuck. Ten years I've been your Friday night fuck. Ten years you've been fucking the Russian."

"So you've said." He yawns.

"I'm definitely dating others."

"Good. Meanwhile, get some sleep."

I wake before he does. I wake anxiously. It's six a.m., and Josh is in my kitchen fixing my towel rack, making a mess. Sleepily, I make breakfast, setting the table that faces the bay. A low stream of fog lies over the bay, and foghorns blow lonely.

7

He tightens the molly bolt. His sleepy hair sticks up and his clothes are rumpled. A rain of dandruff speckles his dark blue blazer. His rimless glasses are smudged. He glances at his watch. "I have to get going."

"Of course. To her. Your za-za boom."

He sighs impatiently.

"Go to your exploding stars and get it on with Miss Russia."

He slips on his still-damp trench coat and rushes from the loft. For a long time, I sit by the window, watching the fog float over the city, deciding that this time for sure I'm going to meet other men. I don't want to end up ten years from now in the exact same place. No way.

After Josh left, feeling really crummy, I decide enough with the case histories, it's time for true love, to put myself out there. I hurry to my office, my coffee beside me, and I go on line to BoomerBoom.com, type up a profile, post a glam photo, and spend the next couple of hours checking out boomer men.

For the next couple of weeks, I have several phone conversations with new men, take notes on the ones I want to meet and meet a few at the local bar or at Starbucks. So far no one is interesting to me, but at least I'm out there. And still, I believe that my fate is set and that one of these days I'll turn and he'll be there.

BELLS OR BALLS?
SETH SOMMERSTEIN

Tonight, Seth the furrier picks me up in his black Mercedes convertible. I've gone out with Seth twice so far. The top is down, and it's freezing. Of course, he's bundled in a black cashmere coat, and a cashmere scarf is wound around his thin neck. I'm shivering, plus my fifty-five-dollar blown out, long hair is flying around like loose wool, and I'm terrified my contact lenses are going to pop out. Plus, he doesn't help me with my seatbelt, and I'm pulling the strap, feeling like a moron and sucking in my breath, until finally it clicks into the metal slot. Frank Sinatra tapes are on, and Seth sings along to "The Lady Is a Tramp," glancing at himself in the car mirror. *Hello,* I want to say. *I'm Katy, Your date. Remember me?*

At a Middle Eastern restaurant, the kind with gold-gilt doors and sexy Middle Eastern music and belly dancers clustering along the walls like silk scarves, he orders apple martinis inside huge red glasses, and these spicy kabob things on a stick. Thank God, I took my IBS medication. Spicy food will put me away. So anyway, we're sprawled on these humongous satin pillows, my hip killing me, and these gorgeous belly dancers are gyrating in front of him. He's sticking folded twenty-dollar bills in the dancers' waists, winking and acting as if he's King Boomer hotshot. Feeling no pain, I'm attracted to this moron; we've got the mojo going. I'm on fire, doing this Bette Davis thing—shaking my hair, dropping my wrist, and pouting my Armani red lipstick lips. He's blowing in my ear, then complaining that his dead wife was not only "a klutz," but frigid, and would only let him have sex on Monday nights.

"A dead fish," he says, looking melancholy.

He sighs, looking morose. "You're the first seventy-ish woman I've ever been attracted to. I want to make love to you."

"I love PETA," I say.

"I'll order some," he replies.

"Not bread! I'm against killing animals for furs and rugs and coats."

"Too bad. I was going to give you a gorgeous leopard bag."

"No thanks."

"I want sex with you," he says.

"I know," I say, thinking, he's a jerk but I'm sexually attracted to something underneath his glib gab. Something about him. *Thank God I'm wearing my new Victoria Secret red lace underwear.*

He glances at the gold Rolex watch. Looking panicked, he stands. "Excuse me. Gotta take my diuretics."

"Sure. Gotta do what you gotta do," I say, knowing that he's going to the men's room to take his Viagra.

Fifteen minutes later, he comes back to the table, looking like the cat that swallowed the canary; he thinks I don't know. The belly dancers are going wild, their bodies floating like silk scarves, their skirts stuck with money.

"Let's go to my place," Seth says. "I want to show you my wall hanging from India."

He lives on the twenty-sixth floor. His co-op is all beige with wall-to-wall windows. Leopard skin pillows and fur and animal rugs cover the dark hardwood floors. A telescope looks out at the fog and blank air. Ultra contemporary furnishings are fabulous but seem displayed.

So vulnerable, I think. *And he turns me on.*

In his enormous white bedroom that looks like a Calvin Klein underwear ad, he lights these tall incense candles, and the flames rise like a campfire. What's worse is that above his bed is a humongously huge oil portrait of a blonde woman lying on a bed. It's his wife, he whispers. He clicks some buttons, and the drapes open to the moon and this sad-sack Indian music plays. His awful bulldog Harry, with nasty eyes and bad breath, sits on his pillow, glaring at me.

Quickly, we undress. He poses a second, showing off his perfect naked body with not an ounce of fat. I'm glad it's dark, glad he can't see the pouch under my stomach.

"You have beautiful breasts," he says, as if he's uttering the secret to the Holy Grail.

In bed, we get right at it. At first, I'm nervous, but thank God, he's hard and goes inside me. Okay, we're hot kissing like bandits and the guy is hard as a brick and doesn't have hip problems, though he's on the small side. The butterflies are going and I'm feeling the thrill of new sex with a new man. But he's a talker, one of those instructor types, shouting, "Fuck the dick, baby. Pinch my nipple. Love your fur." Plus, he's hard of hearing.

"You're hot, too," I shout into his ear.

We're going pretty good, and my legs are wound around his neck like rope, and he's fucking so hard that I'm praying that I don't pee—I pee when I cough or feel pressure—but I'm feeling hot. I mean, the oldie can fuck—when suddenly he pulls out.

"I'm not going to get pregnant! Keep doing what you're doing!" I shout.

"Balls," he instructs, laying on his back now, his legs and arms spread as if he's on the crucifix. The music is rising.

"Bells?" I ask.

"Balls! Can't you hear?"

"Where are they?" I'm on my knees, looking around.

"Are you blind?" he shouts.

"I have cataracts."

"God, suck the balls," he frantically shouts.

Bingo. I feel these tiny marbles that he thinks are a gift from God. Please, God. Let me get this done. Blood rushes to my head. Then finally, as I grab one pea-sized ball into my mouth, he's screaming like a moose in heat. His life alert bracelet goes off, and there's pounding at the door. Medics burst into the co-op, stethoscopes swinging from their necks, and they push me aside and are all over him like a cheap suit, giving me dirty looks. His thingy is still hard, and I'm groping for my clothes, and his ugly dog Harry is yelping and clawing my bare legs. Half-dressed, I run out of there, the neighbors in the hallway pointing at me. I get the elevator and rush into the street, calling, "Taxi. Taxi."

All the way home, I keep my eyes on the moon. It seems so close, so unobtainable, yet it's mine, all mine. Only the moon appeases me. Was it always this way? Romance? Sex? Or is it that we're older and the oldie guys think there's no need for romance? Is it possible in this Viagra generation?

Damn the moon. Damn how beautiful it is. I want it all, the moon, the sky, the one. What good is sexy sex if the emotions aren't there? Then it's only performance, replacing past desires…

ON THE PHONE WITH
BOOMER HOTTIE FRIENDS

"One ball I touched, and it was over! So this morning, I called the furrier's house, and his housekeeper Sari said he's in the hospital. She said it was my fault, and she hung up on me."

"Sandy already told me about it," Marcy says.

"It was a nightmare. All he wanted was for me to lick his balls."

"These guys with their balls," Marcy says, sighing. "Yuk. What's the big deal?"

"Like chewing bubble gum."

"I agree."

"My face was down there for hours, and the balls were so tiny I couldn't see them."

"So the moron was masturbating on you."

"All night he complained that his poor dead wife was frigid."

"They all say that, sweetie. Jeffrey says the same thing about his dead wife. Poor thing jumped off the bridge—"

"Not to mention an earring was on the furrier's nightstand, and he tried to give it to me. He couldn't even remember whose earring."

"Memory loss, sweetie."

"So are we just like old dogs in heat?" I ask.

"Dogs don't have the problems we have. They do it, bark their heads off, and then move on to the next. Thank God, I met Jeffrey. I'm in love. The sex is off the chart—"

As Marcy continues to talk about the "great sex" she has with Jeffrey, and what a "genius performance artist he is," I fight the urge to tell her that I think Jeffrey is a pretentious jerk, and that I'm terrified he's going to soak her for all she's got.

Marcy is a sixty-two-year-old, beautiful, successful fashion photographer; her photographs are in French *Vogue* and top fashion magazines all over the world. Her last husband, a ninety-two-year-old, world-famous real estate mogul, died sitting on the toilet and left her a fortune. We met twenty years ago at a posh gallery exhibit of Richard Avedon's photographs. We've been friends ever since.

Beeep.

"Get your call. Gotta jump. Talk later…"

"Niki, hi," I say. "I was on with Marcy."

"Sandy just told me that the furrier had a heart attack. These boomers with their balls and sex toys. Sandy said that poor Bunny Blumenthal got a sex toy stuck up her ass and had to go to the doctor. Disgusting. Today on the show, I interviewed—"

Niki Cortez is sixty-four, Hispanic and African American. She's stunning and produces *Niki Says*, a talk show on the Hispanic local television network. She's a well-known activist for human justice, and we met years ago at a political rally in favor of same-sex marriage. She's never been married, and at a routine eye doctor appointment, she recently met Dr. George Williams, a drop-dead gorgeous, African American, sixty-year-old ophthalmologist and jazz singer.

14

"So tonight, George is taking me to dinner and dancing at Yoshi's. He wants me to meet his daughter soon—"

"Don't hop in the sack yet. Give him a run for his money. He sounds like a keeper."

Beeep.

"Take your call. Gotta run. I'll call you tomorrow." Niki gets off the call.

"Lorraine, hi. I was on a call with Niki."

"I hope she plays it cool with George. She won't be meeting the daughter if she sleeps with him too soon. No matter what generation we're in, they like the chase."

Lorraine Swenson is sixty-nine, six feet tall, Norwegian, with pale blonde hair and ice blue eyes. She won a silver medal for vaulting in the 1960 Olympics. She's a well-known poet, known for her poetry on spirituality. She has been married twenty-seven years to Wong Wang, a wealthy CEO of a start-up company in Silicon Valley. They don't live together, and they date others, but Lorraine never divorced him. He showers her with money and enables her to pursue her art and help other women artists. "I'm the wife, heir to Wong's fortune. No other bitch is going to take it," she always says. Several years ago, I met Lorraine at a poetry reading at Niki's fabulous house in the Mission, and we became friends. I really like her.

"Niki told me about poor Bunny Blumenthal. She's got to stop trying to please these boomer freaks. Now you can see why I don't divorce Wong."

"Gotta go," I say, glancing at the clock on my wall. My next patient has arrived. "I have a session in ten minutes. Love you. Talk later."

I dim the lights in the office and spray the air with the special gardenia scent I bought in Japan Town. I meditate for three minutes, and then I open the door and greet my next patient, a retired root canal dentist who is grief-stricken about his recent divorce. He's short with a small head and a tuft of curly hair. He has a long, thin nose and sultry eyes. He sits on the leather couch facing me. I take my position in my black leather chair.

He begins. "I've always loved bitches. And she's a bitch—"

DICK JACOBS

This dating is a nightmare, but I force myself to continue dating. No way do I want to give in to Josh. Anyway, again, I believe that one's fate is set, and it has its own agenda and journey. I assure myself that meeting new men will lead to "the One." Plus, for my research, it's always interesting observing the male boomer generation. It's amazing, but so many of the boomer men I meet, from fifty to ninety, have developed great financial and intellectual resources, but on an emotional level, they're stuck in the old generation where men still think they're Tarzan and you, Jane. They're just not developed. But I still believe in love.

So, this rainy Thursday afternoon, after my last patient, I arrive at Starbucks. As usual, I sit in the back, facing the door. I sip my iced decaf Americana with an inch of soy foam on top and take notes on my Apple MacBook Air. In ten minutes, I'm meeting Dick Jacobs, a famous seminar leader of How to Find the Right Partner. He'd read *Boomer Heat* and emailed that he wanted to meet me. On the phone, he sounded sassy, smart. Quirky. I'd seen him lecture on PBS television and was impressed by his rhetoric and support of boomer women, so I decided meeting with him might be interesting. If he's really true to his work.

The café is busy with men and women working on their laptops and iPads and talking on their smart phones.

Exactly at four, this huge man wearing a Harvard sweatshirt hurries towards me. In person, he looks different from his glossy press photographs. He has a mass of high, puffed, salt and pepper hair, suspicious eyes, and critical, thick lips. We shake hands. After he gets his organic peppermint tea, complaining of a "gassy stomach," he sits next to me.

He looks at me intently. "You look pretty good for sixty-seven," he says in a deep radio voice.

"Either you look good or not. What does age have to do with it?"

He sips his tea and intently looks at me, sitting in a shrink way—zombie-like. "You're angry at men."

"Wrong. I like men."

"Hey, lady! Your book is angry! You're not Freud! You make boomer men sound like retards! You're pissed off at men. You need sex!"

"I'm not angry at men. I—"

"You older women lie," he continues unpleasantly. "They say they're fifty-five, and I meet them, and they're ninety-two. They have back problems, knee problems, humps on their backs, and they're looking for a schmuck like me to take care of them."

He pauses. "Netflix?"

I nod. "I love film."

"Thank God, a woman who knows film. My third wife, Ilsa, was twenty-seven. She thought Betty Davis was Betty Boop." He pauses. "She ran off with the gardener, and after he left her, she died from a ruptured appendix."

"Shame."

"Are you on anti-depressants?"

"No."

"Most of the boomer women I meet are on anti-depressants. Their hands are ice cold, and they're catatonic."

"Sounds like you don't believe what you preach. I've seen you on television."

He shrugs. "In my business, people don't want to hear the truth." He pauses, looking at me intently. "Are you Jewish?"

"Is the pope Catholic?" I reply.

He laughs, revealing even, slightly yellowish teeth. But there's something vulnerable about him. He's got all the signs of insecurity. I'll give him a chance.

"Do you want to come to dinner tomorrow night? I make a mean pot roast."

I hesitate. "Sure. I'll try your pot roast."

The next night, I'm in a taxi, on my way to Dick Jacobs's house. The driver is yelling in some foreign language and driving like a maniac.

"Please, sir, I just got out of the hospital and— Please don't drive so fast."

"Hey! You Americans are pussies!" he shouts, turning around and glaring at me. He drives even faster, up and down hills, and I'm doing my meditation shit, repeating the mantra I use on airplanes or inside elevators.

Finally, the taxi stops in a narrow alleyway on Russian Hill. I pay the driver and hurry up the hill, careful not to get my five-inch Prada heels caught in a pothole. The alley is narrow and the street slants up. "Look for a red door," Dick had instructed and then, *voila!* I see the door.

I ring the doorbell, and after a long moment, the door opens. Dick looks great, decked in a blue cashmere sweater and snug jeans.

"You look…great," he says, his bulging eyes scanning my black, stretchy, off-the-shoulder, long-sleeved Anne Klein dress.

He leads me along a narrow hall, past posters of himself with stars who attended his seminars, into a cozy living room. Tango music plays from a stereo inside a bookcase.

I sit on a long beanbag type of couch. Incense candles are lit everywhere, and tons of books are in bookcases, on chairs, piled on the floor. Autographed pictures of himself are signed and arranged on a wood table.

"Vodka. Straight up," he says, pouring vodka into a glass. "Three green olives."

"How did you know?" I ask.

"I know a lot about you."

"Are you analyzing me?"

"I already did."

"We're even. I analyzed you, too."

We click glasses, as if we have a pact. I gulp the drink, feeling more relaxed. We shoot the breeze about our careers; I dream of writing a novel about a seventy-year-old ageless woman. He brags that he's going to be on Oprah. "My ratings are higher than Dr. Phil's," he brags.

"My Los Angeles agent wants to option *Boomer Heat* for a movie based on my case histories, kind of like that movie about Freud—"

"The public doesn't care about a bunch of fucked-up boomers," he says unpleasantly, looking at me suspiciously.

"I disagree. Our country treats age as if it's a disease, and that's the reason so many of the boomers have age anxiety and neuroses. Our country makes anyone over fifty feel like a throw-a-way. We're labeled senior citizens, boomers, and given ten-percent discounts at Ross. I hate it. We're not treated like people with dreams—"

With a sullen shrug, he says, "Let's eat."

The pot roast is dry, but I'm eating like a horse, trying not to gulp or make clicking sounds. If I chew too hard, my bridge clicks. A few years ago, I fell on the street and lost some teeth, but got this great bridge. Anyway, we're talking a storm about books; we love, Nora Ephron, and Faulkner.

"I'm wild about Hemingway and Fitzgerald."

He shrugs. "They were drunks."

"I love Hemingway's work. It's elegantly raunchy. Everything in his work is so complicated about relationships—sexuality. Also, I think *The Great Gatsby* is the world's greatest novel."

"Gatsby was a horse's ass. Mooning after that bitch Daisy."

"Men still love who they can't have. Fitzgerald's issues still exist," I persist, aware that he's looking cranky.

He blows out the candles, and a heavy spiral of smoke wavers and then curls into the air. "Let's have a brandy in the living room."

The fire is going big-time, and Ravel's "Bolero" is sensually rising. *You know what that means*, I say to myself.

"I prefer Bach," I say. "Glenn Gould plays Bach like no one else."

He whispers, "I'm hot for you. I want to take you to Calistoga for the mud baths and the Glenn Gould Bach Festival. I want to have fuck weekends, to do nothing but fuck—"

"What about love?" I ask, pulling away. "Isn't that what your book is about? Finding love?"

"You Jewish older women want it all!" he shouts, getting all red in the face. "You're never satisfied with a pot roast and an orgasm! We want different things!"

"I just meant—"

"Meant that you want it all!" he shrieks, his eyes bulging. "That's what Ilsa meant! She took everything! I was pussy-whipped! All you women want the same thing. You older ones with sagging asses and social security checks want it all!"

He's screaming and ranting in detail about how the "bitch Ilsa," did him in, how all women do him in, how he's "tired" of taking care of women. No wonder he can't find the "right" woman, he repeats. "They're all bitches."

I get up and put on my jacket. "Well, the pot roast was…great. I have to go. Have an early session tomorrow."

"Stay," he coaxes in a solicitous tone. "We'll watch some great French porno films. I have a twenty-seven-inch plasma TV in the bedroom. I'll show you happiness."

I call a taxi from my cell phone. "I have a case history to write."

"What are you writing about?"

"You."

I rush into the night. By now, the mist is thick, and I feel rain. I love the rain. It promises so much.

Midnight:
On The Phone

"*C*an you imagine, Sandy? The freak cooks a lousy pot roast and thinks that I'm going to fuck the night away."

"Hey! Honey! Not too shabby! At least he wants to fuck. The boomer-plus men I meet are wearing diapers. If they cough, they fart; if they walk fast, they pee in their pants."

"This guy was a competitive, nasty prick," I continue. "I've had it with these dead wife freaks. They act as if they're at a party, popping Viagra. Plus, this Dick Jacobs freak told me his dead wife was frigid, yet he keeps her ashes in a schmootzy jar."

"Chemistry, *schmenistry*," Sandy says. "These boomer guys want everything. The sixty-year-old drummer I've been flinging with says I need more Botox. During sex, I caught him staring at the lines on my forehead. Like he's such a beauty. His face is a prune."

"No Botox for me. I think it's terrible what women do to themselves," I scoff.

"Bunny Blumenthal got her vagina botoxed, and it puffed up like a watermelon. She had to go to the ER. Not to mention that she has so much Botox in her face her teeth are bucked, and she can't close her mouth. She got seizures! Worse, she was giving the astronaut a blowjob, and her hair extensions got caught on his zipper and he saw her bald! He hasn't called."

23

"Since Josh discovered that swollen star behind Jupiter, his female graduate students treat him like King Cock. Plus, the man doesn't bathe."

"He looks schmootzy," Sandy laughs. "I know the syndrome; I was married to the great Jewish doctor who was cheating on me right after we'd have sex. Not worth it."

"Professor Cock-a-Doodle-Doo thinks I don't know that he's fucking his twenty-five-year-old Russian graduate student, Helga. A real bitch. Spiked hair, heels like knives; she looks like a James Bond character. She's doing her thesis on Jupiter, using Josh for his money and his clout. She moved right into his schmootzy house with her ninety-year-old mother from Siberia, and Josh tells me she's a tenant!"

"Once you dump the schlump, you'll find your love."

"All he gave me the past ten years was herpes and bladder infections. I've had it."

Beeep.

I have nightmares that I'll have a stroke and my forty-four-year-old daughter, Nanny, and her husband will have me carted to a convalescent home, and I'll be sitting in a deck chair in the hallway with dirty hair and thick glasses, drooling, a Velcro nametag pinned to my floral robe from Costco.

I stare at the moon. It's extra bright tonight. Revelations come from deep regrets and bring the past up close. I'm glad I've been in lousy therapy for thirty years because now I know each regret as I know my shoe collection. It's great to feel the present; each moment is so exciting that sometimes I feel like the ground under me wobbles.

Roger Berman

"I'm a catch, the ladies tell me."

Roger Berman uncrosses his legs, a sign that he is upset. I wait. A siren goes off outside, but I keep the windows shut and the drapes closed. Roger doesn't like any light. It's hard to get him to probe himself. I listen to clues about what he doesn't say—his sudden pauses and long silences when his mother is mentioned. So far, what I've come up with is that he's sexually frigid and fearful of his sexuality.

"Gloria is allergic to my cats. She gets allergy shots, but she still breaks out in rashes. On top of everything else, she doesn't make a lot of money."

"She works very hard, you said."

"I want a woman who makes a lot of money. Who doesn't want my money."

"Does Gloria? Doesn't sound that way to me."

"I told her that unless she quits her job and earns more money, I can't see her anymore. I'm not her cash cow. I take her to expensive restaurants. For her birthday, I gave her a Rolex watch. She thinks I'm King Farouk."

"Sounds like you like her."

He presses his lips into a thin line. "She's not great in the sex department."

I remain quiet. I wait for him to talk. He's dressed like a count—couture fitted jacket, silk scarf around his neck, snug couture jeans, and Gucci boots. He's perfect looking, up to the minute in style.

"I told her that I'm not sexually attracted to her. That I don't want sex with her."

"But you have sleepovers. Why?"

"She can't be without me. She stays on her side of the bed."

"Uh-huh."

For the next thirty minutes, he rants about how fabulous he is, the money he's made, his sailboats, Crystal Cruises, the young girls he dates, his singing. "The women love it when I give them my CD."

He reaches into his coat pocket and takes out a CD with an airbrushed glamour shot of him leaning against a piano. Printed in bold block letters—"*Bliss*, by Roger Berman."

He takes clumps of Kleenex. "I don't want to get old. I don't want to die. End up in a jar like my poor wife. Our dog knocked over the urn and ate her ashes. Who needs it? Who needs old?"

"Why do you see Gloria, then?"

"She's nice. I feel sorry for her."

A siren went by. Two more minutes. I lean slightly forward, count to ten. "Unfortunately, we have to stop."

After he leaves, I write in my case history. I write:

The emotional intelligence of a ten-year-old boy. He has inflated dreams of fame and beauty queens. Deflated self-image. He's with Gloria because she takes care of him. She's his mother. He hides behind his money, cars, couture. All his life he has lived an unlived life, hiding his sexuality.

26

What am I hiding? *Not my sexuality, but something even deeper. Something like the person I pretend not to be. The part of me that never felt romantic love.*

Why? When I try to go deeper in my analysis with Dr. Bruno, I've never been able to go there. Instead, it's like a flat, gray plane with no air, as I imagine space is.

THE DAUGHTER

"Okay, don't yell!"

"I'm not yelling!"

"You're yelling!"

"It's my ear. I can't hear well!"

"Mom, you need to check it out. Between the cataracts and the ears, it's time to find a boyfriend."

"I go out!"

"With freaks."

"I'm trying!"

"Get rid of the schmata professor! Ten years you've been with him. Before you know it, you'll be in a nursing home, folk dancing with the pathetics! You better hurry up."

"Thanks for the memory."

Silence. Nanny is breathing hard. She's forty-four and married to a fifty-one-year-old architect she met on Match.com who'd never been married. She spent the past several years living with him until they married. Now she thinks she knows everything about men. She's so sweet, but she's always bossing me and giving me advice on how to be with a man. Her father never paid attention to her, was too drunk, and at an early age, she was taking care of me. Role reversal, but I'm trying to be more assertive.

"Okay, Mom," she sighs. "I hope you have a good time with the next one. My husband and I pray every night."

"Well, pray for rain. It's a better bet!"

Beeep.

Josh:
Boomer Commitment-Phobic

This time I didn't call Josh. It's been weeks since we talked. Josh calls. He calls and hangs up. He thinks I don't recognize the broken beep on his old cell phone, or the sound of his breathing, like quick gasps. He calls again. He says, "Hello, this is Josh."

"Yes. I know who you are."

Silence.

"I—"

"Don't say it, Josh. It's over."

"Don't be a fool, Katy. What we have is never over. You know I love you."

"You have a girlfriend!"

"Not really," he sighs.

"Not really means you do, freak!"

Silence. Heavy sighs. Now comes the silent treatment.

"All right, I have a girlfriend."

"I knew it. Ten years I've been with you. I know everything."

"But I don't have sex with her that . . . much."

"'That much' means you fuck her! You'd fuck a snake with a bag on its head!"

"She's more a companion."

"What am I? Your sex object?"

He sighs heavily, in an irritated tone. "Ten years. Every Friday night, I pick you up at seven on the dot."

"You take me to a lousy Thai dinner—I hate Thai food! Still, you take me to Thai food, and while I choke on the lousy noodles, you rant about your exploding stars, then you have great sex and go home the next morning!"

"Sounds pretty good to me," he chuckles.

"You're a freak!"

"So you've said."

"You think because you're a hotshot professor at Stanford that you're a genius. I'm done! Don't call me anymore!"

"So you've said," he sighs.

I bang the phone, bang it twice to make sure the receiver is in place. This man gets to me. I'm shaking. For a while I sit like a goony bird, looking out the window, watching a low veil of fog float over the city.

BOOMER HOTTIE GET TOGETHER

"*I* dumped the schlump!"

"Josh is a schmootz ball." Sandy pours Kettle One vodka into her shot glasses. Her blonde streaked hair is expertly cut blunt and swings as she talks. She wears a low-cut black jersey dress that accentuates her voluptuous curves and a shocking pink silk scarf wrapped around her rather short neck. Mid-calf, black, simple leather boots complete her look.

We're at my loft. It's Friday night. Every week, we go to each other's houses and then to a club or to dinner, sometimes the theater. We're drinking vodka shots, eating Brie on wheat thins, and updating each other on our careers and goals, and then of course, the talk changes to our dating lives.

"Women get into bad habits," Marcy says, sprawled on my white leather Barcelona chair.

Marcy's very curly, black, shoulder-length hair is like a cape, striking against her very white, flawless skin, very red lips, and gray-shadowed, black, romantic eyes. She wears a black cashmere off-the-shoulder loose Versace top, black slim slacks, and fabulous, high-heel, crimson lizard ankle boots. A band of silver gracefully wraps around her long, slim neck.

"All of us, no matter how progressive we are or how old, want romantic love," Niki states. Niki's gorgeous caramel skin glows. Her chestnut-colored hair is parted in the middle and arranged in a low chignon at the nape of her long neck. Her eyes are the color of cat eyes—yellow with black rims.

We're all talking at once about women in the new, ageless generation. How we had to transition from one generation to another. Some of our sisters from our past generation never moved forward, and they're living the same as their mothers had. We agree that to keep youthful, you have to move forward into the new generation. Traditions are marvelous, but moving forward takes more than traditions. It's setting new goals, new traditions to mix with the old, consistently delving into your self. Staying back makes one strangely old.

"And I've had it with the age thing," I say. "Sixty is not the new forty. Sixty is the new sixty!"

Lorraine lifts her glass for another toast. She wears a long, black Chinese coat over black leggings and high heels. Her almost-metallic gold hair is swept back from her face, and a huge jade ring is on the forefinger of her right hand.

"These boomer freaks aren't emotionally developed," she states sadly. "We women had to develop in so many ways. Also, so many of the older boomer men have suffered from cardiac arrest, prostate problems, and impotency. They try to make up for it with young girls, showing off their money and sex toys. My twenty-eight-year-old son treats his girlfriends' right. I see to that."

I say, "As Meryl Streep says in the movie *It's Complicated*, I finally feel normal."

"Poor Holly Barnblatt," Sandy says after a reflective silence, wrinkling her nose. "She's still with Walter. The freak gives free How to Get Rich classes at his penthouse to meet women. While poor Holly, a big-time criminal lawyer, sits in his stupid classes, watching him flirt with these twenty-year-old losers. Sad."

"Sad what many women think they have to do to keep a man," Sandy argues vehemently. "I've been there. Done that. My Jewish doctor ex-husband was a rat. Cheated on his first wife. But I thought it'd be different with me. Once a rat, always a rat. After the divorce, I went to Israel and joined the army. I learned a lot about women. Strong women."

Sandy's dozens of bracelets make a clicking sound. Deep dimples indent her full cheeks.

"The older boomer men are caught between two generations," I muse. "They haven't moved into the new, ageless generation."

"As we have done," Niki says exuberantly. "We weren't born to technology, to our roles of breadwinners, CEOs, and advanced education. I was a reentry woman, and so was Katy, and a single mother on top of it. I was the oldest reentry woman at UCLA, working two jobs to get through graduate film school."

"Amen," Sandy says, popping a shrimp puff into her mouth. "We're all reentry women. We'd been programmed to be the little women at home, to take care of these freaks. They don't want us now. They want youngies to replace their dead wives, ex-wives and to take care of them. They reward them with lavish lifestyles."

Lorraine says animatedly, "Look how women artists and writers were treated, and it's not so great now. Joan Mitchell, when she was in art school, the male head master told her, 'Your work is so good the public will think it was done by a man.'"

"I hear you," Marcy says. "It's the same with photography. Though fashion is better."

"I'm paving the way for Nanny to pass the torch. It's like a relay race. You can't stay stuck in one generation."

"We're fabulous!" Lorraine says. "Let's drink to us!"

"To everything is possible at any age," I say.

"Here, here. Now let's go to dinner, then tango dancing!"

Time passes. I miss Josh. But I continue dating. The dating is tiring, and I take copious notes about myself. What is it that I'm always without a love partner? Never was I any good in my marriage, or even love affairs. When I examined my past relationships, closely, I see that I always constructed walls or chaos or something that would suddenly end my relationships. No matter how much therapy I've had myself, that glitch is in me. Do you ever eradicate such glitches—fears of love, rejection? Anyway, I'm busy with Boomer Heat and my career. And I love my profession and my lifestyle, so why isn't that enough?

I close my computer and turn off the lights. It's time to dream.

NANNY THE DAUGHTER

"The schlump will be back."

"Nanny, that's not true. I ended it."

"That's what you said ten years ago."

"Give me a break."

"Mom, you're a hot lady. What do you need that schmootz bag for? For an orgasm? Watch a horny movie. If you'd handled him right, you could have him, too, with all his schmootz."

"You think you know."

"I know!" she shouts. "Look how I got my husband. Do you think I got him by nagging, confronting, and then going back on my word?" She sighs heavily. "Mom, I want the best for you."

"I have the best. I love my work, my sister friends. I love my life."

She sighs again. "Mom—okay. We'll talk tomorrow," she says in baby talk. "Oh, Mom, maybe a dance class would be good. You're always with those depressing sickly patients and your girlfriends, and their depressing relationships—"

Beeep..

Boomer Clean Freak

I'm at a book signing at Apple Inc, this posh bookstore and wine bar. Josh calls sometimes four times a day. He calls and hangs up. He sends postcards with drawings of stars and little poems. He even, for the first time in ten years, sent flowers. He knows my favorite flowers are lilac roses. He sent red carnations, but still, he sent flowers.

Since I'm not seeing Josh, I'm forcing myself to attend all the events I'm invited to. I have a tendency to be hermetic, stay at home, work, and talk on the phone with the girls.

Anyway, my sixty-two-year-old friend, Deidre Applegate, gave a reading of her new mystery novel *Kill*, about a serial killer. The small bookstore is full of Deidre's groupies and wanna-be writers. They wear black, long, tangled hair and neon-colored backpacks.

I'm in line, waiting to pay for my book. And as soon as I can, I'll sneak out and hail a taxi home, looking forward to watching a re-run of *Amadeus*.

"Aren't you Katy? Katy Roseman?"

I turn around and face a small man elegantly dressed. About my age, his thick mane of silver hair sticks high up, like those troll dolls. He has snappy, dark, critical eyes behind rimless glasses and an odd kind of sex appeal.

"Aaron Shapiro," he says, extending a large hand. "I'm the food critic for *Fame* magazine."

"Yes. I've read your books on restaurants around the world."

"I love *Boomer Heat*. Your case histories are interesting. Very Freud. Only you skewer men."

"I do?"

"Skewer," he repeats, as if to no one, smiling and revealing veneers so white they glow.

For a while, we shoot the whiz about editors and agents.

"It's all on E-books now. Any schlep can publish a book." He sighs impatiently.

"Well, that's good. We live in a different world. There is no age. Everything is possible."

"A fucked-up world. Food poisoning is rampant in our country, and I'm researching the best restaurants."

"I know," I reply. '' I'm afraid to order lettuce. Plus, I have, well, a sensitive stomach."

"My wife was a chef."

"Wow."

"She died from a bad radish in a fancy schmancy restaurant. My new book *The Radish* will be released next year. It's going to knock the socks off the friggin FDA in our country. They sell sick cows to butchers, produce with feces on it." He pauses. "My poor wife. She was a pistol."

"Shame," I say. I glance at my Walgreens underwater watch. "Well, good luck. I have an early morning session—nice meeting you."

"I want to take you to Coo Coo for dinner, tonight. It's a five-star restaurant, and the food is unique and *clean*."

"Clean, yes."

"Clean," he reverently repeats. "My wife was clean as a pin."

"Pins are good."

"Let's go." He frowns. "We can talk then. A therapist and a hottie. Interesting," he says, as if talking to himself. He takes my hand and leads me to the parking garage. He aims this remote thing in the air and all these weird sounds go off. "You see? Hear that one whale like sound? That's my car."

We're in his black, shiny SUV. Food journals and menus and trade magazines litter the front seat. He drives between two lanes, his small body crouched low in his seat. Opera tapes are blasting loudly, and the windows are shut tight. He's yakking about salmonella and what a terrible death it is, and I'm getting depressed. Plus, at stop signs, he sprays this antiseptic stuff and then wipes his hands with these friggin hand-wipe things that stink like Clorox. I'm gagging and my tear duct is watering. I can't breathe.

"Can you open the window, please?"

"Bugs."

"Bugs?"

"Bugs are everywhere," he says, his voice rising. "I can't open the window."

"I don't see bugs."

"Honey, you can't see them. They're in the air. They're all around us. The last woman I was with let her sheets go for a week, and I got bed bugs."

One of those Howard Hughes freaks. Why am I here? I hate his too-neat Gucci suit, too-neat car, too-shiny Gucci shoes, and too-white teeth. I hate that at every stop sign he puts his cold, clammy hand on my knee.

I hate the restaurant. It's too serious. Drab. Military. Gray fabric walls, cranky looking waiters who speak only French and move as if they're gliding. I hate the endless wine. I'm dying for my vodka straight up, hate the tiny courses, huge plates with a tiny mussel floating on it, flowers on top of the soup. While Aaron's slurping up the food, he's raving about how his wife was one of the top chefs in the world. "Honey, she was on Oprah, won awards. She was a pistol."

"A pistol and a foodie. You were a lucky man." On his smart phone he shows me a video of his poor wife in the kitchen, cooking.

"Fabulous," I say.

"Clean as a pin."

"So you said."

He stops eating and looks at me as if looking at me for the first time. "You're… interesting. You border on the weird, but you're fun. You look a little like Annie Hall."

"Wow, uh-huh."

He proceeds to tell me about the array of "bad blind dates."

"If they're beautiful, they're dumb; if they're homely, they're too nice. If they're rich, they're bitches. You can't win. That's why I haven't remarried. My wife was clean as a whistle. These women aren't *clean.* They wear dirty underwear."

When we leave the restaurant, as the valet helps me into the car, to maintain my balance, I place my hand on the car.

"Oh, my God!"

"God what?"

"You *touched* the car!"

"It's just…smudged."

Now he's crying. You got it. He's crying, ranting that he just spent "two thou for a friggin' paint job!"

He takes pictures of the smudge with his cell phone. Then sprays this stuff around me to keep the bugs away.

ON THE PHONE

"Bugs. All Mr. Clean talked about were bugs."

"These boomer oldies are nightmares," Sandy says. "Their wives spoiled them." "A lot of these boomer guys are stuck in our old generation. They think we're the same little woman at home and want us to lick their balls, make tuna casseroles, and clean the toilets. They don't know we moved on. We're not that generation."

"Lorraine told me last night that the latest with poor Holly is that her freak Arnie won't have sex with her because she reminds him of his mother. Hello. He's gay. He hasn't had sex with her in fifteen years. He treats her like she's his assistant."

"Pathetic. She's an abused woman. Gay men are fabulous and don't act like that! She should dump him."

"Of course, she should, but now that she's in her sixties, she's afraid she'll be alone. She has to have a man in her life."

"So anyway, Aaron Shapiro was interesting, but all during dinner, I had to hear about how fucking 'clean,' the wife was. Her bout with salmonella from a rotten radish—that she bathed in antiseptic. She probably died from Clorox up her pussy."

"I had Mexican food with this fifty-five-year-old hotshot politician from Mexico I interviewed on my show. During lunch at the top of the mark, all he did over his Cobb salad was complain that he was born with a tiny penis but knows what to do with it, and only wants tall and rich women. He spent the entire time questioning me about my finances. Twenty-two years out of Harvard and this is what I deal with! No wonder I'm in love with George. Only, he's starting the freak-calling thing. As soon as we had sex, he stopped calling every night. Shouldn't it be the other way?"

"Well, now he's worried you'll want more, so he's backing off," I say. "It reeks of an issue. But see what happens. Be who you are. Stay cool."

"For sure. So far, he's got a lot of special charms."

"At the Jewish over-sixty singles hop, I danced with an ugly retired seventy-year-old tree surgeon," I continue. "Poor thing had a huge hump on his back, and I didn't know where to put my hand. You could hang a coat on it. He sang 'Old Man River' in my ear. Even ugly men are jerks. No wonder I miss Josh. At least I know what I'm getting. He's promised to spend weekends with me if I take him back."

Niki laughs. "Honey, we've got each other."

Beeep.

"It's Lorraine. Back from Finland. Sandy said that the schlump called again. Knew he would."

"He's begging me. He promises that he'll change."

"He'll beg until you fall into the same routine again."

"I'm on a call with Niki. Can we talk later?"

"Okay, see you Friday night. My house."

I miss Josh. I play Philip Glass, watch my videos of Josh lecturing on PBS about the universe. I miss his schlumps, his sexiness. When he makes love, he becomes someone else. Then we're the only two

43

people on the planet. But is that enough? Enough what though? Do I really want more? Of course you do. Or are boomer women trading old husbands and boyfriends for maybe different issues but for the same man?

Boomer Hoarder

Earl Philips is a fifty-nine-year-old pharmacist. He owns the huge pharmacy where I buy my Lipitor. He knows a lot about medications, and everyone goes to him for everything.

Several months ago, his wife died, and he became even friendlier. We talked about politics—both of us raving Democrats—and our love of poetry. Then he invited me to see a film on Pablo Neruda, and to dinner. I always liked Earl, so I thought why not? I'm still holding off Josh, and besides, I need more material for the sequel to *Boomer Heat*. Anyway, Earl has watery, romantic blue eyes, pale blonde, wispy hair, and a soft, literary manner.

"I read Ted Hughes's *Birthday Letters* and cried through the whole book," I say at dinner. "It's a love letter to Sylvia Plath. Before I decided to be a therapist, I studied Plath."

We're at this Ethiopian restaurant, and over bitter coffee and sticky honey cakes, we talk for hours about literature. I'm enraptured by his insights and knowledge.

"I want to read 'The Waste Land' to you. Let's go to my house."

I nod. Wow. I feel like I've met Prufrock.

So on the way to his house, he drives across town, reciting poetry, and I'm really turned on to his poetic, gentle, Richard Burton-like voice. We're talking Jane Austen now and just the way he recites lines from her poetry, sighing, then moving on to Sexton—his range is exciting, and I'm on fire.

At the top of a steep hill, fog devouring a narrow wood house, he jerks his Volvo to a stop. I follow him up these tilted stairs to the top. He explains that his house "shifted in the last earthquake," and the steps are "slightly off."

"How interesting."

"Voila!"

He opens the door, and the air smells like rotten eggs. Then he turns on the light, and, oh my God, he's a hoarder, the kind you see on television: boxes, clothes, bags, computers, and clothes piled to the ceiling. I'm dumb founded. Isn't there anyone normal? How can someone so literary, gentle, be a hoarder?

"Since Meryl died, I haven't been expecting company," he says after my first gasp. "But the bedroom isn't bad."

He pulls me along a smelly, dark hallway, slushing over piles of books and garbage bags, into a room that stinks of old boxes and rotted fruit. He turns on the light. Even worse, the light illuminates the maze of fruit flies, and piles of papers, books, clothes, and paraphernalia (still with price tags), stacked to the ceiling.

"How do you—"

"Live here?"

I nod. "Rats, do you have rats?"

"Mice, but the exterminator handles that," he says impatiently.

He pushes stuff from the bed onto the floor.

"After Meryl died, I slept on a futon in the next room. I never wanted to sleep in our bed—until tonight."

"How did she die?"

"She suffocated in her sleep. I think she had a heart attack."

"Uh-huh."

"In memory, I don't touch her things."

"Really, I have to go."

"Stay. We'll read 'The Waste Land' together." He's pushing things off the bed, not caring that boxes are spilling onto the floor.

"It's been great. Gotta go," I repeat.

I run down the stairs, wondering if any men after fifty are normal, and flag a taxi.

The moon is bright and I stare it in the face, determined to find forever love before I die in a hospital bed with Dr. Phil reruns on the television. The moon is beautiful. So bright. There's a man in it.

I'LL TRY HARDER—JOSH

"I'll try harder."

"That's what you said last time," I reply.

"I want you back," Josh says, on the phone.

"Because I'm not emotionally available. That's why," I reply.

"Part of it." He sighs. "I'm a sick bastard, but I miss *you*, Katy. I want to spend more time with you. It's been months."

I hold the phone tight.

"Please, Katy. Let me see you next weekend. I'll stay the entire weekend. Saturday, we'll see the new Woody Allen film, then go to dinner, then I'll stay overnight, and Sunday we can go to the MOMA and see the Cindy Sherman show."

"I don't want to go back to the way we were, Josh. I'm over that."

"I mean it this time, Katy."

"Maybe dinner. Just dinner."

"I'll pick you up tonight. Seven."

Exactly at seven p.m., Josh stands in the doorway, looking nervous and, as usual, schlumpy, though I can see that he had washed his hair—the curls puffed on top. He wears his usual tennis shoes, nice new jeans, and black blazer, dandruff sprinkled on the shoulders like confetti. But my heart melts when I see him. We kiss nervously, gushing how great we look. How great it is to see each other, acting like stumbling teenagers.

48

"Drink?"

"No," he says nervously. "I have something for you. A small gift."

He gives me a small silk box, the kind you buy in Chinatown. Inside, there's a tiny picture of an enamel sapphire blue star with radiant orange light.

"I give you Eta Carvinae."

"I'm speechless. It's the most beautiful star I've ever seen."

It's the largest star in the universe. It's 7, 500 light years away, and has the most brilliant light."

"It's beautiful."

He puts it around my neck.

"Josh…"

"Don't get syrupy. You know I hate that."

"Thank you."

He unrolls a coffee-stained paper, squints his eyes, and reads, "John's North Beach Café, I hear, is excellent. You love Italian food."

"Let's go." I put on my black fedora and my black pea coat.

The restaurant is one of those great San Francisco mafia-style restaurants—white linen tablecloths, napkins, old waiters wearing starched white coats, black and white tile floors, the smell of pasta and whiskey. It's dark and discreet. We sit in the back, and we drink vodka shots.

"You look lovely tonight," Josh says romantically.

I hold his hand. I love his hands. They are large, strong hands. But he bites his nails to the quick.

"So what's happening with your work?" I gulp my third shot.

Josh tells me about his coming trip to Paris, where he'll give a paper on star clusters, groups of stars that are bound by gravity.

"Are they dying stars?"

"Everything dies. They are very old stars. Death is inevitable to anything living."

"Do you think after death we go someplace wonderful in the universe?"

He shrugs and looks melancholy. "I think death is death. It's over. So make your mark while you're here."

"I think there's another journey. There has to be."

"I know. You believe in aliens, and psychics, and ghosts."

Josh continues to talk about his view of the universe and his love of the stars. When he talks about this, he becomes someone else, full of wonder and radiance and expertise. Not the usual bumbling womanizer. I love him this way, and I find myself weak to his charms, even telling myself that we could live the rest of our lives together, working and looking at the stars.

"All sounds fascinating," I say, enjoying the raviolis.

To top it off, this violinist plays a love song and the night, the music, the stars, and—I'm a goner.

"Katy, sounds like your work is going well."

"My film agent in Los Angeles thinks he'll get a movie option on *Boomer Heat*."

"You want the stars and the moon and all of it."

"I do. I won't settle again. I do. I do. I do."

He kisses the palm of my hand. The heat from his mouth shivers along my body.

At home, it's almost midnight. We had after-dinner liquors at the bar, and I gushed while he continued to talk about star clusters.

"Well, it was great. I had a wonderful time. Thank you again for my star."

He takes me in his arms, and we're kissing and really kissing, and then we're kissing passionately, a little voice warning me to stop. I pull away. "It's late, Josh."

He sighs heavily. "Where is the little red toolbox I bought you a year ago? I'll fix your dishwasher."

"It's late, Josh. Not tonight."

From the window, I watch him hurry across the street to his new smart car. Of course, he'd have one of those things. He likes gadgets and toys. I watch until the car sputters away and for a moment longer, I watch the stars blinking in the dark sky, some bulging and ready to explode.

Like love.

NANNY

I love winter. It's near the holidays. The air is crisp, and the fog is cold. I love winter because it's romantic and promises new journeys. I feel invigorated.

Today, I'm at my desk writing more case histories, when the phone rings. I'm writing about Steven Nankin, a fifty-eight-year-old, handsome trust fund baby. He has never worked. He thinks he's dumb. I write, *He's oblivious to the fact that during our session he plays with his genitals. Gets up frequently to wash his hands. Goes to singles parties almost every night, but has never had sex.*

The phone rings. It's Nanny, who has been upset that I'm seeing Josh again.

"But Josh has been fabulous," I insist. "He stays an extra day. He said he loves me. This weekend, he's staying the entire weekend."

"Mom, don't be a fool—"

"I'm not! What's wrong with having happiness?"

"Don't shout!"

"You're the one who is shouting!"

Silence. Breathing.

"You sound like you have a cold," I say after a long silence.

She sniffs. "I'm okay. I miss you. When am I going to see you?"

"Tomorrow," I say. " I'll drive over tomorrow. We'll go to Chungs for lunch…talk."

"Okay, Mom. But I advise you not to see Professor Schlump. He's not going to change."

"Well, I'll see what happens."

Beeep.

"Hold on."

"Katy, it's Sandy. Niki flew to Cuba with George. I'm afraid for her. When he was taking a shower, she looked through his cell phone and saw one number frequently. It's a woman."

"They all have women until the one."

"There's never 'the one.' It's always about them."

"It's about us. Numero uno. Gotta call you later. I'm on with Nanny."

Beeep.

THE AGENT

"Lovey doll," croons my Hollywood agent. "We have a firm television option on your columns. The network thinks *Boomer Heat* will be a terrific reality show."

"I'm not a housewife of Orange County. I'm a therapist with a book about serious case histories."

"Lovey, there's no money in movies. Also, by the time the studio makes it, you won't be on the planet. Trust me. Hollywood is a slow boat to China. You know that."

"You said a movie. I don't want a reality show."

"*Want?*" she shouts. "Who cares what you want? There's bucks in this."

"How much for the option money?"

"It's a free option. Be grateful."

"Free? I don't do free."

"Honey, you're pushing seventy. I told them you're fifty-one. Even that almost killed the deal. We'll get you some Botox. Get those boobs lifted. Be grateful," she repeats. "The major movie studios won't put money into someone your age. There's no value, no longevity. A reality show could be a legacy."

"It's ageism!" I shout.

"Lovey, stop with the age shit. Hollywood doesn't like to hear about age, but Dick is a major movie producer, and you should meet him. See if you can talk with him."

"Dick who?"

"Fuck face Al Kahn. He's smart, but a dick. All the nebbie Jewish guys are executives and dicks."

''Uh huh,'' I murmur.

"It's *de – lic-ious*.," she continues. ''Al Fuck-face is a genius. He is the first to do a conjoined twin reality show. He wants you in LA for a meeting."

"I'll only meet him if he'll do a movie. But let me think about it."

"Gotta jump."

Tonight, the fog is rolling in. I love the fog, its beauty and coziness. I catch up on my case histories. The wind-bells on the tall windows make a gentle clanging sound. I love the sound of the wind mingling with the low bellowing sound of the foghorns. It's late, but I like working late at night, when it's quiet. I like the quiet. I open the file cabinet and take out the large leather journal that I keep my current case histories in. I write them by hand. I like to do that. It helps me think better. Later, I have my assistant type them up into files.

I open the ledger, and for a while, I write about George Berman. He's been making headway, but very little. *Gloria serves as his surrogate mother, but his affection runs deep for her. Why does she stay? Because from what I know, her father abandoned her and her mother died young. Deeply, she's more fearful of George's abandonment than not having his love. Abandonment wins out: His fear of entrapment, of being "caught," that he's bi-sexual, keeps him in her warm, unconditional love. Her fear of abandonment keeps her from wanting sex with him. So the two are working. If I can only get George to recognize this without falling apart—it's delicate.*

I sip the espresso coffee. I think about my own abandonment issues. I think about something that I haven't thought about for thirty years, something as deeply embedded in my psyche as a child buries a pebble into the sand. I was nineteen and a virgin. I was programmed to marry the highest bidder. This is how middle-class Jewish girls were programmed. I married Charlie Berkson, a twenty-eight-year-old, handsome tycoon who'd inherited his grandfather's oil business. Money was no object. I was thought to be the luckiest girl in the world. My father mortgaged his house to give me a huge, fancy wedding. On my wedding night, in the moonlight, eager to end my virginity, I was all over him—only he pushed me away. He lit a cigarette and said he'd made a mistake, didn't love me, "couldn't do it," and took me home the next morning. From then on, I'd lived in a silent kind of disgrace and shame.

I write, *Dr. Katy Roseman's case history: First page:*

After the annulment, in which Charlie claimed I was frigid and a fraud, like a glove inside out, I turned deeply into myself, where I lived alone with my imagination. I'm hidden, too. Not in my sexuality, but in my dislike and suspicion of men. Maybe that's why I've never experienced real love and intimacy. Stayed with Josh.

In real life, I only pretended to function, learned what Mother called "charm," learned to please, to do the right things, but no one knew me or saw me. Least of all myself. Only in glimmers. I was deeply afraid of rejection. Repeat the same kind of relationship, only with men who are sure to hurt me. Why wasn't this clear before, why didn't I notice, even when I was married to the drunk and to a man who was drunk all the time and who beat me too many times? Then, just as I was to leave him, he dropped dead. I am deeply terrified of true love and joy.

I'm hidden, too. As the smell of smoke lingers long after a fire, I give off an aura of 'don't get too close.' I know this now. Suddenly, it's so clear.

I write for another hour, until the foghorns stop. Josh provided me great sex and the fantasy that he'd be different, but like Gloria, I was in love with his potential and always knew he'd never reach it. That he was stuck in his own fear of entrapment.

At the window, I watch the lights from the lighthouse drop gold ripples along the dark and foreboding ocean. The East Bay Bridge is lit with lights and sculptures that gleam like a diamond necklace. I feel a sudden surge of joyful energy. Any bit of self-awareness, acknowledgment, like a dark fog lifting slowly to light, reveals a new layer of joy.

Later, I paint flowers on a black silk dress that I bought at a bazaar. The flowers are black, green, and yellow.

PART TWO:

TRYING TO FIND LOVE, FAME, AND FORTUNE

THE WORKOUT

"Mom, you have to get in shape," Nanny advised. "Also, keep dating."

"I am. I only see Josh every other week. I've been busy. He's away a lot."

"Away where? To Jupiter? He's always away giving papers on his fucking stars. Who knows what he's doing?"

"Anyway, I joined Crunch."

"Good, Mom."

Anyway, this is my first day at the gym and I'm assigned a trainer, as I paid extra for a twice-a-week personal trainer. Saturday Night Fever plays from huge speakers, and the place sounds like a disco. Good-looking boomer men and women pump iron, their lips clenched, their bodies posed like body builders.

"Hi, I'm Debbie, your trainer."

"Hello, Debbie. I'm Katy."

"It's De-be, accent on the second e," she explains. "Like Demi."

"Sure, uh huh."

About twenty, and wearing a teeny red tank and teeny-tiny shorts, she shows me the ropes on the treadmill. Her eyes are baby blue, and her silky, pale blonde hair is held back by a baby blue headband. Even her nails are painted baby blue. In a teeny-tiny voice, she lectures the advantages of good bodybuilding, looking at me sympathetically. As a child watches a clumsy mother, she helps me onto the treadmill, explaining how I need thirty minutes of "cardio."

"Sure."

"At your age, it's imperative to get your heart rate up."

"Sure."

Her valley girl voice sounds like Kim Kardashian—this indolent, lazy, valley girl way of speaking—a question at the end of each sentence—so annoying. She instructs me how to stand, with my "shoulders back."

"Sure."

"We'll get that flab turned into muscle." She pats the slight sack on my stomach.

"Uh-huh."

"I'll turn it on for thirty minutes," Debe says, setting the timer. "If anything goes wrong, press the red button. I'll be back in thirty minutes."

I'm walking on the treadmill, my hands clenching the sides. This humongously huge Russian woman is on the tread next to me, running fast, and every few seconds she grunts and shouts, "Hey!" I'm running faster now, my breasts bobbing up and down. God, I hate this. I'm out of breath. Why am I so out of breath? I eat organic vegetables and fruit and get plenty of sleep. I don't smoke and only drink socially. On my left, a woman with long silver hair and arms that dangle like stems is running. We start gabbing it up. She introduces herself. "Jamie."

"Katy."

"First time?" Her small breasts barely bob, and her skin is very tanned.

"Uh-huh," I say breathlessly. My nose is dripping snot, and why aren't I all neat like she is?

She confides, "After my divorce four weeks ago, I decided to get the body in shape. I'm dating a teenager," she whispers. "He's got these great abs."

"Wow."

"I'm sixty, and lying down, your body flattens out, but sitting over this piece of a an Adonis, I could die. Everything hangs—"

She continues to talk off my ear about "blowing" the "teenager," who repaired her running toilet, how "hot," he is, that they're "fucking like rabbits," and how "boring," her husband was.

"Wow," I say, running faster now.

"He's a hick, has one ball, but who cares? The sex is great."

"Uh-huh."

She returns to running while on her smarty-smart phone. I'm running faster now, but I'm tired, and the treadmill is going too fast, and I'm getting tired, so I reach for the red button, but I lose my balance and I'm going backward, and I slide off the machine onto the cement floor.

My knee is bleeding and no one stops what they're doing to help me. A humongous man with tattoos up his muscular arms, lifting weights, just glares at me. Even Jaime is still on the phone.

"Are you all right?" De-be asks, suddenly by my side.

"The treadmill was too fast."

She looks at me with Bambi eyes. "I'm sorry, dear. We can't go slower. You need to get in shape. Eat lots of broccoli—"

"Broccoli, yes."

61

"I'll sign you up for the slow Pilates class. Get your strength up."

"Uh-huh."

"Go home and rest and we'll see you tomorrow."

"Aren't you going to look at my leg? It's swelling up. It's—"

"Ice. Put plenty of ice on it," she yawns.

Slowly, I get up.

Outside, the sun is bright and a breeze sways the rows of trees along the streets. As I walk, my knee is swelling and I feel kind of weak, but I'm glad to be alive without a broken hip, assuring myself that I'll exercise and get in shape without the gym. I'll walk the hills and notice how the clouds form formations and fog drenches the city like pink chiffon.

SEPARATE CHECKS

Meet Paul. He's sixty-six. A news journalist. We've known each other for years. We met at a seminar on how to market your book. He'd published *Writing Correctly*, a book about grammar. He's never been married.

He's slight, vain, and fancies himself a Gregory Peck double. He buys thrift shop dramatic clothing and often dresses like Sam Spade. No car. He takes buses everywhere and often on Saturdays, we meet for the Indian food buffet. He's nice, schleppy, but smart.

Today, Saturday afternoon, we're at the Indian restaurant on Polk Street for the all-you-can-eat lunch buffet. He wears a white panama hat with a black band, and a dusty, huge, tan gabardine overcoat.

At the buffet, he piles his plate high with tiers of curry, rice, eggplant, lamb. Then at the table, though he's slender as a weed, he scarfs up three helpings of everything. The poor Indian chefs wearing turbans and white chef coats stand diligently by the buffet table and give Paul irritated looks.

Between huge mouthfuls of curry, Paul complains about his career, ranting that he could have been a "great journalist." He covered Iraq and was almost killed, he rants loudly. "Now the paper has me writing about these dreary San Francisco socialites with their matching couture and French twists."

"Ageism," I say, feeling bad for him. "My book sold only three thousand copies, so now the out-to-lunch publisher won't take my calls. Fuck her. I'll self-publish."

"Good idea.," she says.

"Easy for you to say," he snaps, his mouth full. "You have a major publisher and foreign rights. Hard to believe when your book is full of case histories about fucked-up boomer men, while my book teaches proper grammar and linguistics and no one wants it. The public is satisfied to hear everyone talk like the moron Kardashians." He raises his fist. "I could have been…"

"A contender," I finish.

"I'm a genius," he continues, patting his watery, turquoise blue eyes with a paper napkin.

"It's ageism. Gotta keep your dream. Join me in the first Age March in history that I'm trying to get together. Everyone will celebrate their real ages and protest ageism."

He brushes rice from his rubber-like lips.

"I'm attracted to you. You remind me of Chanel #5 perfume and the white kid gloves of an old movie star."

I smile. He goes on to say that the women in his life are always beautiful. He recites the names of the women he "should have married," how "rich" they were, how "friggin gorgeous," still stuffing his face with curry.

"Well, marriage isn't for everyone," I say, feeling kind of crampy, thinking, *Oh, my God, I have IBS, and no, I don't want to use the teeny bathroom in the back separated by a thin, gauze, gold curtain with a tassel.*

"I think I could go for you," he says.

"I don't think so," I quickly reply, not wanting to hurt his feelings. "Besides, trust me, I'm not one for relationships."

"So what are you? A robot?"

"Sshh! People are listening."

"Do you have Medicare? Netflix? Comcast? Supplemental insurance?"

"Sure, I have them all."

"We could pool our resources. Split the friggin' Comcast and other shit. We could collaborate on projects."

"Oh, no. I can't. I don't want to be with anyone. But it's not you. You're smart. Nice. But I prefer to live alone. I don't want that kind of relationship—"

"If you're not one for relationships, why the fuck are you taking up my time?" he shouts, indifferent to everyone looking now. "To use me for your fucking case histories?"

"Excuse me?"

"You heard me! I've taken you to lunches, movies. You're a gold digger. A taker. A user. You use me to pick up your lunch tabs! Your frigid case histories—"

"I'm not using you," I whisper, my hand pushing the air down, warning him to keep quiet. "I enjoy our friendship, learning about grammar, talking about film."

"Are you saying you're not attracted?"

"Not in the way you want."

"Cunt! You're a tease cunt!"

"Sshh. Everyone is listening."

"Let them listen! They can hear what a bitch you are. You can take all your credentials and shove it!"

"Ssshh!"

"Waiter!" he shouts even louder, not caring that everyone in the tiny room has stopped eating and is watching. "Separate checks, please!"

Later, in my office, I write Paul into a case history. *A man full of lost dreams. It's a tragedy not to live your dream, who you are. If you don't love yourself, finding true love is impossible. He seems incapable, unwilling to dive into himself, identify his regrets, then to celebrate himself and move on and pursue his dreams—there's always new journeys, even at the very end.*

ON THE PHONE

"Another freak. Here he was a friend for years, and he's looking for a nurse with a purse."

"They all are. Even the rich ones," Sandy says.

"Because they're men, they think it's our turn to take care of them."

"Sad, but true," Sandy says. "They think the woman's movement is about taking care of them. They think it's because of our menstrual cycles. Morons."

"Isn't there a real man out there? Someone who is ready for the new woman? Women in our generation? The boomer ageless generation? Why do they have to go into the old school generation? Me Tarzan, you Jane. Where is an updated Rhett Butler?"

"Honey, Rhett is probably in diapers."

"But with an intact virility and soul."

"Niki is having outrageous porno sex with George. It's off the chart. She's in love."

"Do you think great sex is love?"

"Absolutely. What else is it? You sound like one of those old hippie bitches who call orgasm love."

Beeep.

"Lorraine, I'm on with Sandy."

"George hasn't called Niki in a week."

67

"Not good. Not a good sign."

Beeep.

"Mom! You didn't call me back! Are you on the phone with your freak girlfriends? All they do is complain about the men in their lives. I'm your child. Call me. I want you to go with me to the Macy's white sale—"

I DON'T WANT TO BRAG
BUT IT'S THE SIZE THAT COUNTS

*N*anny is right. Josh is always traveling to Zurich or Paris to give papers and lectures. I wonder if he takes his so-called tenant Helga. I'm angry with myself for falling into the same pattern with Josh.

Haven't I gotten over my attractions for emotionally unavailable men? I'm worse than some of my patients. With this in mind, I amp up my dating life, assuring myself that I'll wean off Josh. The dating is tedious, but interesting. Like one looks for a penny lost in a sand pile, a part of me is always waiting for that moment when my great love will be there. I never knew what love was—in my fantasy, until I met Josh, but that isn't love. It's lust. Still, I wonder, is there a difference?

Anyway, tonight, I'm meeting Jim Nathanson. He's a sixty-two-year-old widower real estate tycoon from the Midwest that I met at the Museum of Contemporary Art member's party. He'd seemed pretty cool. He likes jazz, contemporary art, and even rides a Harley. Not bad looking—he's fit and has a tuft of pale, tan, curly juvenile hair.

The buzzer rings, and I meet him downstairs in the corridor. He wears a schmootzy navy blazer with three faded brass buttons and wrinkled tan cotton pants.

"You look lovely," he says, his beady eyes scanning my red rubber raincoat and fuck-me gladiator high heel shoes.

"I thought we'd walk to an Italian café on Market Street."

"Sure."

But it's raining like hell. So we walk in this friggin' storm. God, it's dark, and a heavy, cold rain spills over San Francisco, making humongous puddles on the cracked, narrow streets. San Francisco is a mess. No money. The streets have potholes, and the sidewalk slants up in spots. Oblivious to my getting soaked, he opens a humongous, black, Mary Poppins umbrella with a big point on its top and holds it over his head, its edges poking my face.

He walks fast on his rubber shoes, and I'm running along, trying to duck my head under his umbrella, furious that my expensive blow dry hair is frizzing. I hate it when it frizzes. I look like my Aunt Zoë in Israel when it frizzes. Plus, I'm praying I don't fall and break a hip, like my poor friend Dusty did.

At least ten blocks we've walked. Not to mention he's boring, yakking about his motorcycle and that it saves money. All he talks about is money, about all the properties he owns, and that a "penny saved is the road to wealth."

"Does this restaurant have a bar?" I ask, out of breath now.

"Just wine."

He sounds irritated. He has that cranky look about him.

"Do you mind if we stop at a bar? I'd like a martini. I hate wine. Plus, I had a stressful day, and a martini relaxes me."

"I know. My wife was in AA."

"I'm a *social* drinker," I say, feeling defensive.

"Here's a bar," he says crankily, leading me into a small dark bar with sawdust on the floor and jukeboxes lit up like candy. These muscular young guys with humongous tattoos on their necks and arms are at the bar, playing liars' dice and betting beers. A jukebox plays Britney Spears songs. Anyway, we sit on the stools, and I order a Stoli vodka over ice. He doesn't drink, Mr. Sad Sack says, with a frown. He orders a Pepsi with lemon. Our drinks come, and like pulling a prize from the bottom of a Cracker box, he takes his time pulling the exact change from his wallet.

"No tip for this guy," he mutters, frowning.

I gulp my drink, feeling immediately lightheaded.

"Do you mind if I have another? The drink was watered down," I whisper.

He frowns. "Another for the lady," he reluctantly says, opening a leather coin purse and slowly taking out the change.

The jukebox is playing country Western songs. I'm nursing the watery vodka, trying to engage him in conversation, but mostly he frowns or nods his head, which is somewhat large for his body. He sips his Pepsi, yakking about the days when he was an engineer building fisheries in Alaska, how much he loved his wife, who died from liver cancer.

"She was a runner-up beauty queen in Minnesota," he says, a wistful expression on his face. Then he tells me about a woman he met on JDate. "She owns two condos and also has a series to the opera."

"Sounds good," I say, thinking he's a jerk.

He frowns. "Owning property is *important*."

"I own my loft, if that's what you want to know," I say, trying not to slur my words.

He frowns, pressing his rather small mouth. "Why do you live in a loft?"

71

"Because I love it. Because I see my patients there. Because I paint."

"No one earns money in therapy." He frowns, looking at me as a disgruntled parents looks at an unreasonable child.

"I do. Plus, I have a film option on *Boomer Heat*, my case histories."

"Sure," he says nastily. "You're just getting famous all over the place."

"Say, I'll have another vodka. S tress," I repeat, not caring what he thinks.

"That's what my wife said." He nods to the bartender, who places another watery drink in front of me.

Now he's telling me that his blissful wife was a "drunk," ranting that she "fucked up her liver," and about the years of AA meetings.

"Shame," I say, gulping my drink.

"This dating business is hard," he says in an exasperated tone, looking away as if having a conversation with himself. "I'm selective. The older women want my money to supplement their social security. They pretend they're rich, and they don't have a pot to pee in."

"Shame."

"I'm very *careful*," he adds, now looking at me like a parent warning her child not to go near the edge of the water. "I know that I have a lot to offer. Most of the men my age are wearing diapers." He pauses, blinking as though he's prideful. "I don't want to brag, but it's not the size that counts."

"Uh-huh." Does this mean he has a tiny one? she wonders.

He touches the side of my face. "You're very beautiful in this light. Like a young girl," he says, his mouth close to mine. "I'm not sure where this will go, but I find you… interesting."

"Whoopee," I say, gulping the rest of my drink.

"I haven't slept with a woman since my wife died two years ago. I'm willing to try."

"Do you have a new bed?"

"Of course not. It's the same bed my wife and I shared for thirty–seven years. A perfectly good bed. You can't buy mattresses like that anymore. A penny pinched is a penny saved."

"Uh-huh." Cheap too, I think.

He grabs my hand and places it on his small, erect penis. So small I can barely make a fist. "I beg your pardon. Sir, take my hand off your penis, please."

"I want to show you up front that I'm not built like a horse. No secrets. As I said, it's not the size that counts."

"I'm not feeling too well. I'm going to catch a taxi and head home—"

I'm home. I sit on my deck, watching the moon slide behind the dark. Why does love seem so elusive? Only existing in great novels or films? When I look back at my marriage, I clearly see that it wasn't about love. No, it was about provision, being married in time to birth a child, to have a role, an identity. By the time I knew this, I was unhappily married, and I spent my time and years back in college pursuing a career and a profession as a psychologist. By the time I got the Ph.d, the husband dropped dead.

But now, when I dream of love, I inhale roses and imagine our hearts beating together.

The phone rings. I have it on speakerphone. When I hear Josh's voice, my heart skips a beat. "Baby, I'm home from Zurich. I'll pick you up at seven tomorrow night."

He coughs three times, pauses, the phone drops, bumbles strange sounds, and then clicks.

THIS TIME IT WILL BE DIFFERENT

"Do you hear me? I mean it this time! You're still fucking the Nazi."

Josh coughs three times. He looks pale. Thinner. He's been traveling for the last month.

"You said this time it will be different. So what's different? You're away all the time. You still leave at dawn, and you're still fucking the Nazi. I know it."

"You *know* everything!" he shouts. "You think you *know* everything."

He's furious. He buttons his shirt, the buttons crooked. He dresses fast. It's six a.m. Saturday morning. I'm furious.

"I know you. I know that when you shut down your phones, you're fucking her. When you're suddenly sick with your stupid allergies, you're with her! First, it was with the Russian whore; now it's the Nazi bitch. Your twenty-five-year-old graduate students. You freak."

He sniffles. "Katy. Please. I'm an old man. I don't feel so good. Don't shout at me."

"I've had it with your sexual glitter. You're all about sex. All about glitter. No integrity. You're like your friggin stars, all pretty and shiny, but ready to explode and evaporate at any minute. I want more than what you want."

He coughs four times, then makes this gargling sound in his throat.

"You're not listening!"

"I have a tickle in my throat."

"Buy a cough drop! We're done. I'm done. Do you hear me? After ten years, I'm done!"

He sneezes.

"Go. Get out and go to your Helga. Leave me alone. Go."

"Katy, please don't. I'll see you next week, Katy. You know I love you."

"I don't know any such thing. Go."

He clumps across the room to the front door. When I hear the door slam, I get up and go to the window. It's raining, and I make a circle on the window, like a hole, to observe him as he sluggishly crosses the street to his car, which is parked in a loading zone. He grabs the big white ticket on his window, fumbles with the door, then gets into the car. He drives away.

An hour later, I call Sandy. I confide that I have mixed feelings about Josh.

"You're penis-whipped with him, honey. That's all it is. He's a schmuck. Get out of it."

"I'm trying. It's not that easy."

"Or go on the Dr. Phil Show. He'll give you hell for being with someone who won't give you anything on your terms."

"It's not that easy."

"You're a great therapist, and you're letting yourself be stuck. You won't meet anyone as long as you're with him."

The rest of the day is cold and gray. I spend the day in my office, writing case histories. I write notes about Roger Berman. I write:

He is an enigma. Slowly, his story is revealing itself. With him, I work from the outside in. Consistently, he talks about things—expensive technology, his expensive Mazarotti, Coop, summer home in Paris, art, clothes. What he doesn't like about Gloria. Yet he's with her, gives her money, treats her like a CEO paying an assistant. I look for a clue that will bring me inside. Just as I have to in me, to see why I'm still with Josh—

My thoughts turn to Josh: Any kind of entrapment makes him run. He was the ugly, nerdy genius in school, the kind the girls ignored. Now the brilliant, Nobel Prize-winning astronomer, he's in demand. Like a kid with candy, he can't get enough sex. If you get too close, he's cruel. He's a very good father to his grownup sons. His ex-wife ran off and then died.

The reason I'm hooked on him, too, is that he arouses my sexual stuff. I was raised to be frigid and to use men for provisions. Also, my parents were ice cold. Blah, blah, blah—

A Little Botox
You Could Be A Doll!
Dr. Ian Gold

The holidays pass. I had a huge party at my loft and invited everyone I know, except for Josh. I haven't taken his calls. New Year's Eve, I went out with the girls. We went to a gay bar and danced all night. We had a blast.

My new year's resolution is to finish my sequel and take acting lessons. Clean my closet, and forget Josh.

Anyway, today I'm at Starbucks, meeting a boomer cosmetic surgeon that I met on BoomerSingles.com. He said he's interesting. Anyway, we're at Starbucks. Poor thing has a hump on his back so huge I could hang a coat on it. Plus, he has black, shoe-polish dyed hair and a face so done you could slide on it. He gave up his practice and opened a Botox center. He wears green hospital scrubs, and a stethoscope dangles from his scrawny neck. His eyeglasses are huge, aviator-style, and outdated, and his skin is pulled so tight, I can see the veins.

"Lillian, you're a lucky man. When did she die?"

"Eighteen years ago." He sighs and looks wistful. "I used to sing 'Love Story' to her. She loved my voice."

I lick foam from the top of my decaf cappuccino—two shots, dry inside, and tons of foam.

"She was a beauty. I did her face, and they say she looked like Jane Fonda."

He opens his wallet and gives me a frayed photograph of this woman in her late forties, maybe, with a face so done she looks like a mummy.

"Very bling," I say.

He sighs heavily. "No offense. You're nice, but I'm used to great beauties."

"I can see that."

He wiggles his nose. It's very red at the tip. "I like to communicate. I'm a communicator. Doc, we make a good team. You fix souls and I fix faces."

"Well, it takes more than that," I say.

He sighs. "The women on the Internet are all liars and felons. The blind dates I meet are throw-a-ways looking for a handout."

"So why did you answer my ad?" I ask, after a long silence.

He shrugs. "I like women who have professions. I scanned your book. Very interesting. I have a *fabulous* life story, and I thought you might use it for one of your case histories."

"I only use case histories of patients I work with. I take my career seriously. My case histories are a study."

He narrows his eyes. "Isn't it too late to be Dr. Freud?"

"Too late? I'm just warming up."

He frowns. "Say, you look good for sixty-eight," he says, squinting his tiny eyes at me. "A little Botox and you could be a doll—definitely a forehead lift," he says, his face close to mine, blowing his sour breath on my face. "Your eyebrows are low…lines on your upper lip—" He pauses, as if continuing with his evaluation. "Are you a dominatrix?"

"I'm Jewish," I reply.

"This isn't Latin, honey. Top or bottom?"

"Are you one of those nuts with whips and chains?"

"You'd look good in leather," he says.

"Hey! I'm outa here."

Friday Night With The Girls

We're eating seafood at the Water Front restaurant at Pier Seven. The restaurant is hopping. It's Friday night, and the place is buzzing. We're seated next to the window, the ocean is turbulent, and the East Bay Bridge is lit like a diamond necklace. Niki, wearing a beige, cashmere fitted dress, her dark, silky hair flowing down the back, is glowing. We've had several drinks, and Niki is telling us what a great night she had with George.

"Tell us details," Lorraine demands. She sips her bloody mary.

Niki blinks, looking flushed. "I'm not going to tell you about our sex life."

"She's in love," we all say, clicking glasses.

"But he doesn't call for days," Marcy chimes in. Black Indian feathers are braided into her chignon. She wears a white, long-sleeve jersey and skirt.

"He's busy with surgery."

"Bull crap. Not calling is not a good sign," Lorraine says, looking concerned.

"Did you hear about Bunny Blumenthal?" Sandy says. "She was giving a blowjob, and her neck was so high up it got stuck and she had to go to emergency. She's wearing a neck brace."

"Poor Bunny," Marcy sighs. "Here she went and got that stupid dragon tattoo on her ass because the freak said tattoos turn him on."

"Trick is no blow jobs until you have the ring on your finger," Niki snorts.

"Ring or not, I'd rather suck an ice cube," Lorraine says. "I call the shots. That's why Wong and I are still together. Even though we haven't had sex in years, he knows which side of the house is his. I set the limits. I'm his legal wife."

"Some of the most successful, strongest boomer women I know give up their integrity to please a man.," I argue. ''It's okay to please those you love, but not to give yourself up. We have to set an example for the next generation. We're all human beings."

"Not according to men!" Sandy says. "We're chattels. We're still on the planet to please them. They get the firewood, and crouch behind a bush and push out their babies."

"It's getting better," I say.

"Not over sixty. We're still treated like throw-a-ways, and you know it. When television presents a series about a woman over sixty they treat her like she's a joke. It's not real. It's vaudeville."

"Yes, I agree," I say vehemently. "Age is feared in our country. Age racism is rampant. I've had it with the network babes chanting sixty is the new forty. Fuck them. Sixty is the new sixty. I like who I am. I like my age. I like that God is allowing me to live long. Until women stand up for themselves and their creativity and smarts, the men won't change. Some of these women will blow any penis to have a man. They think if they're over sixty without a man they're freaks."

"Yet, you still see Professor Schlump," Lorraine sighs.

"Hardly at all now," I say sheepishly.

"You live once. Poor Holly Barnblatt fell in the street, broke her hip, and now she's in a nursing home. Complications, and her lousy kids stuck her there. We need to live life to the fullest."

"Let's drink to that."

SEXY SEX WITH A STRANGER

I'm at a party honoring Bay Area therapists, at a Victorian house. Wall-to-wall people jam the narrow, high-ceiling rooms. The men have beards and know-it-all eyes, and the women wear stilettos, shawls, and no makeup.

"Hello, I'm Rake Evans," says this tall, cool-looking man with red, wavy hair and piercing blue eyes.

"What an odd name."

"My father was a gambler," he smiles flirtatiously. "He named me after a well-known gambler who'd rake up millions in a night. My father wanted me to do the same, so he named me Rake."

"Did you?"

He laughs. "I'm a psychologist. We don't rake up millions."

Rake wears a thin gold band on his wrist. He's stunning and has the aura of a slow, lazy cat. We make small talk about the function. He practices Zen, travels to India twice a year, and is a vegan. He loves his work.

"I specialize in treating narcissistic older women."

"Are you one of those creepy therapists who have sex with their clients?"

"Never. Only in fantasy."

"Look what happened to Anne Sexton. She got even more fucked up having sex with her analyst."

He shrugs indolently, his probing eyes never moving from my face. "I have a neurosis, Doc. I'm turned on by older women. Especially accomplished, attractive, quirky women."

"Why?"

"First, they know who they are. Second, most older women have missed out on great sex, and I provide them with it."

I laugh. "You're honest."

"I like your crazy hat. High heels—style."

I'm on my fourth vodka shot. I find myself sexually coming on to him. This is unusual for me—usually I play games, wait for the man to pursue me. I had a fucked-up past and distant father thing. But here I am, tossing my hair, swaying my hips, being sexually aggressive.

We continue talking about our work. I confide, "My patients are traumatized about age. Especially the men."

I stand so close to him I can smell the mint on his breath.

"Most of the women I treat are frigid. They don't know about sex. They think it's something to use to catch a man. They use the word commitment. They don't know what it is."

"What about love?"

"You sound like Marjorie Morningstar. Good sex is love."

"But intimacy, partnership—"

"All the things that suck the sex out of romance."

"Have you ever been married?"

"Marriage is highly unnatural. It's a contract, like buying a data plan for an iPhone, and you're stuck with it. It's not conducive to romance or high power sex."

"I do believe in undying, soul-connecting love."

"We'll go to my place." He looks impatiently at his watch.

"Shouldn't we go out at least twice? To a symphony? A couple of nice restaurants?"

"The outcome will be the same. Enjoy your bliss earlier."

I laugh nervously. The audacity. I can't believe this is happening. I feel as though I'm reading an erotic romance novel. But why not be a slut for the night? Explore sex without Josh? As though we made a decision, I follow Rake to his white Jaguar parked in front. Fog floats along the streets like a romantic mist.

He lives in a nice house on Union Street. A garden of climbing orange roses is in the front. Inside, the walls are filled with books and awards. The rooms are tastefully decorated with furnishings he collected from around the world. He loves to travel. He's traveled around the world. He sees patients in a pretty room. There are tons of dark primitive abstract paintings on the wall. "Paintings by my patients."

"Nice," I say, liking his reverent tone when he speaks of his patients.

I follow him down a long hallway into a bedroom. A simple room with an unadorned bed, a few Japanese prints, and wind bells on the windows that chime, as the windows are open.

"Don't turn on the lights," I say, feeling shy. "This is nice."

He undresses quickly, and his body in the half moonlight is fit and beautiful. Then he undresses me, pulling off my clothes, and we're kissing passionately, and I'm thinking this is what desire is, sexual desire. Wow, it's something.

On the narrow bed, his naked body sprawls over my face, his large cock teasing my throbbing vagina. My legs are spread eagle, and we're fucking upside down, on top, and then I'm riding him like a horse, and I'm letting this stranger lick my vagina, the crack in my ass, and God help me, I can't get enough. Then I have this hot orgasm, my hands pressing his strong, fit body closer to me, closer. He doesn't make those moose sounds a lot of men make, he just moves like he knows his moves, knows his orgasm, knows sex.

When it's over, I feel as though I'm inside one of those great French movies where two strangers look at each other and instantly fall in love.

After a few moments, he lights a thin cigar and silently smokes. I'm lying all over him like a cheap suit, whispering how much I enjoyed the sex, kissing him all over, wow, feeling as if I even love him.

"I can't wait till next time," I say, sighing happily, stretching my body like a cat stretches in a sunspot. "I see what you mean about bliss."

He blows a moody smoke ring. I watch it slowly float to the ceiling.

Suddenly he releases my hand, puts out his cigar, jabbing it like a decision into a huge ashtray, then gets up and begins dressing. He's somewhere else now. Slowly, I find my underwear and my clothes, dressing, assuring myself that it's late and time to go home.

On the way home, he says nothing. At my place, he double parks, keeps the motor running, impatiently gunning the motor. If this is what great sex is, I don't want it.

I hurry inside.

I watch the moon disappear and the fog take over the dark, and I slip into sleep.

THE NEXT MORNING

"I fucked him. I blew him like blowing air into a balloon. I've never been so hot, and he's a stranger. Afterwards he acted like Katy who? Cold as ice. If this is great sex, I don't want it."

"After the big O, they're done," Sandy says.

"All men are not made from a cookie cutter."

"Yes, they are," she replies. "Last month, I met Ian Goldman, this hot realtor who bought ten thousand dollars worth of clothes from me. Mr. Sixty-year-old Cool. He took me to dinner at the Four Seasons. He was charming. Talked the *we* thing—*we'll* do this, *we'll* do that. Haven't heard from him."

"The 'we' guys are the worst," I say. "Women don't do this."

"Because women have genes to please a man," Sandy retorts angrily. "That's why gay couples have better relationships. More committed."

"I was in love big time with a gay man, a painter I met at a gallery opening of Mexican pottery, years ago. We went out often and I even kissed him, stuck my tongue in his mouth, but he wasn't interested. Love is so much more than genitalia."

"Not in this country."

Beeep.

"Talk later, Sandy. It's Nanny's number."

"Mom! Did you feel the earthquake? Do you have an earthquake kit? I worry about you. Do you want to end up in the rubble, half-dressed? I'll get you a kit at Costco." She sighs. "Mom, you need taking care of—"

Beeep.

BOOMER BILLIONAIRE

I'm not giving up on my search for love. Usually I love being alone, staying home, reading or painting or being with the girls, but I've made up my mind to go to everything I'm invited to. I go to the opera with Sandy, gallery openings, poetry readings with Lorraine. I try to see everything, learn more. I even booked a Crystal Cruise to Russia next year.

Tonight, I'm at a fundraiser for the foreign film press. In a loft-style building, hottie gay waiters wearing nose rings and attitudes pass chilled martinis and puffy canapés. Latin music is blaring. I'm decked out in my five-inch platform shoes, my off-the-shoulder black jersey top, mid-calf skirt, and black leather ankle boots. A small black hat with a tiny veil sits on top of my shoulder-length, gold-streaked hair. I make hats. Sometimes I make hats from cardboard boxes, paint the boxes, and put veils on top.

Anyway, I'm shooting the whiz with a lesbian filmmaker. She made a film, *Clitoris Lost*. It's a hit. She's stick thin and seven feet tall, and she wears a cape with moons on it. She's really nice and pretty. She rants about how undeveloped boomer men are and that the older men are totally "decrepit."

"I prefer gay men," I say.

"For sure. But gay men don't want you, honey. What do they want you for?"

After she flies the coop, I'm standing by the bar, feeling decrepit, guzzling another martini, and stuffing shrimp puffs in my purse.

"Hello, Katy. I'm Charlie Zuckerman," says this hunk. Wow. Though in his seventies, if a day, he's got this huge, puffed, silver-streaked hair and a movie-star face. He's dressed like Cary Grant— pin-stripe dark suit, French cuffs. Classy.

"I like your hat. Funky," he says. "Not like the usual older woman's style."

"I'm not an older woman. I'm a woman."

"I just noticed."

"Woo-woo."

He laughs. "I'm president of the foreign film press. I know who you are. I read *Boomer Heat*. I want to make a movie from your material. Those poor, fucked-up boomer guys. It could be like a movie about Freud." He pauses. "I'll talk to Bob."

"Who?"

"Redford."

"You got it going on," I say, dawning on me that I've read about this guy. He's a multi-billionaire who backs big movies. He's never been married and is a man about the globe. Private planes, young models, the whole bit.

"I'm looking for new projects to finance," he continues in his soft, feathery voice. "I'm backing a film in Dubai."

"Wow."

"I'll take you for the opening," he smiles, his calculating eyes scanning my body.

"Do I have to wear a Birka?"

"Sounds sexy," he says.

"So you're kinky?"

"Let's get out of here. I want to show you my etchings."

God help me. How can a boomer billionaire hurt? Also, he's never been married. No dead wife to deal with. Who knows? He might even invest in making a movie based on *Boomer Heat*.

We arrive at his coop next to Coit Tower. Wow. The art collection consists of the usual rich man's art—a boring Motherwell painting, a Lucien Freud, and Kline. Probably his decorator bought the paintings at auctions. Everything looks staged. Piles of shrink-wrapped, huge, expensive art books are displayed on antique tables, like props.

In his brown leather den, at a schmaltzy mirrored bar, he pours brandies in two humongous bowl-shaped glasses. I'm sitting on a brown leather sectional that curves around the room like a slide, drinking brandy. He presses some buttons, and bam, this Moroccan music pops on, real sexy.

He sits next to me, yakking about his private jet, Sotheby's, his homes in Paris, Spain, and Dubai. Then, for another hour, in a monotone, he talks about his friggin' health.

"Doc says I have the body of a fifty year old." He pauses, as if waiting for me to agree. "I told Doc the other day," he continues, feigning modesty, "if I came back in another lifetime, I'd want to be me. He was amazed."

"I bet he was."

He pauses then, as he's about to say something profound. "You know, I've never been sexually attracted to a woman your age."

"I'm not usually attracted to billionaire types like you. You're too slick. Everything looks too manufactured."

"Not everything," he says, taking me in his arms. He's gulping my lips and sticking his long tongue in my mouth, and I'm gagging, and I hear a zipper. Then before I know it he's on top of me, and I feel a wet, soft penis on my leg.

"Hey! Sir, your equipment is on my leg. Do you mind?"

"Do you love it?" he whispers, pushing my hand on his tiny, wet thingy.

"Love *what*? It feels like a thirsty dog's tongue!"

"It'll puff up. Touch it."

I'm nauseous. I'm out of here. I push him off me. "I have to go home."

So the guy stands, his thing dangling like a piece of bologna. He sighs. "I'll tell my driver Mohammed to drive you home."

"Not to worry," I say. "Gotta go."

I rush out of there, and outside I grab a taxi, thinking this boomer oldie business is for the birds. Geez, I've had it. Is there ever going to be love?

KATY ON THE PHONE WITH SANDY

"Flat as a pancake," I say. "The guy acted like he was Rhett Butler. His small thing hung like a piece of bologna. He acted as if he didn't know."

"Honey, he's been blown so much by women wanting his billions, he doesn't know the difference."

"I don't care if I ever have one of those things in me again. All I got were bladder infections."

"Most of these boomer-plus guys want to masturbate on you."

"What about love?"

"Don't count on it," she says. "After forty, the party is over. Unless you want to wear his dead wife's clothes, drive her car, and sleep in her bed. Now it's about the vagina. Be lucky you have one that works. Myra Zimmerman is getting Botox on hers. It's so saggy."

"This is when Josh looks good. At least he never had those problems."

"Josh is a major schlump and a rat! What good is the sex if you have a louse?"

"I want it all."

"Good luck."

Beeep.

GOOGLE

"I googled you. You sound interesting."

"Uh-huh."

"Thank God for Google. You're either Google-approved or not."

"Uh-huh. I googled you, too. You're a famous chef."

"We're all googled. So let's meet."

"Okay."

"The last time I didn't google, the woman I met not only had a walker, she was ugly."

"No one is perfect."

"She lied!" he shouts. "She said she was fifty. She was seventy-five!"

"Seventy-five can be hot, too!"

"Hey! You sound hostile!"

"I am to men like you," I reply. "You're an ageist!"

"I don't need this. Either you boomer gals have humps in your back, or you're schizoid. Are you on meds?"

"I will be now!"

Beeep.

ON THE PHONE

"This ageism sucks!" I say to Sandy. "I just talked to an age freak, another boomer down the drain. I've had it with the age thing. These men think we have diseases. Are there any normal people around?"

"Honey, it's age rage. These poor boomer guys are panicked they're going to get prostate cancer, pee in their pants, and can't do it. They have to have the youngies to make them feel whole."

"I'd rather go out with a ninety-year-old man who's cool than a fifty-year-old boomer asshole," I say.

"I hear you."

Beeep.

"Sandy, talk later. It's Nanny again."

"Mom, they're having a bra sale at Nordstroms. Your bras aren't high enough. You need to be lifted."

"I'm busy with patients, and I told you I don't have time for shopping."

"Tomorrow then. Mom, trust me. I'll help you with a makeover. You'll meet the one. You'll see."

Beeep.

ARTH-RITIS?

My back and my neck hurt, maybe from sitting every day, treating patients, and being at my computer. I'm better, but still wearing the foam neck thing. Sandy insists that I go to her chiropractor. "She'll cure you," she insists. Sandy is always running to doctors or an array of Russian healers she swears by, but I agree to try her chiropractor, and Sandy picks me up.

Sandy dumps me into her convertible. With the top down, we drive across town to her chiropractor. Sandy's hair flies free, and her eyes are made up like a cat. I sit like a zombie, the neck thing like a tire around my neck. At every stop sign, Sandy blows kisses to the truck drivers, but when they see me, they make barking sounds.

"Freaks!" she screams, giving the finger.

All the way, she lectures that I have to take better care of myself, eat "organic."

"Sure, uh-huh."

"Look at me! A size four and healthy as a horse. I live on broccoli." Her charm bracelets make clacking sounds, and at every stop sign, she looks in the mirror and checks her vivid red lipstick.

Finally, we get to the chiropractor's office, on the top floor of this hideous building in the Mission district. Huge skeletons dangle from the walls in the waiting room and all these plastic balls are rolling around. Then in comes the chiropractor. She's really butch, huge, and looks like a Sumo wrestler. Behind rimless glasses, her tiny gray eyes are hostile.

"I'm Olga," she announces with a German accent. "So what did you do to yourself?"

"Arthritis," I reply. "My neck is swollen, and my back—"

She squints her eyes. "I fix."

She leads me into this torture room, and gives me a blue cloth gown with a long, thin string dangling on it.

"Take everything off but zee panties. By the count of twenty, I'll be in."

So counting to twenty, trying to undress fast, I get the friggin' gown on.

I sit on the table, and Olga thumps into the room. She assures me to "trust" her. With a hand on each of my ears, she yanks my head to the right, then to the left. I'm in agony. While she hocks about nutrition and vitamins, she continues to twist my head. Then she pushes my back down, pounding it with some hammer thing.

"I'm in agony," I manage to say.

"Old trees sag and bend. You've lost movement in your neck, and you have a bulging spine. You sit too much. You need to ride bicycle."

"Uh-huh," I murmur, tears rolling down my face.

"You not healthy. I make healthy."

She continues to ram my neck about, and what's odd is that now I'm turning my Neck. Amazing. I'm so relieved that I'm shouting that she's a "fucking genius."

"Hitler used to call me to his office. I worked on the Nazi's heads."

"Wow."

She pushes my head more, and an hour later, I can walk without the neck brace. And my back for the first time feels pretty free.

All the way home, Sandy lectures about health, her Russian healers, her psychics.

"That's why I'm in perfect health," she states imperiously.

"Uh-huh."

"I called Tatia in Lenigrad and asked her to heal you. She's working on you."

"What does *working* mean?"

"It means I pay her, and she works on you. She heals people around the world."

"For a fortune. Fraudulent Russian healers are like a virus."

She jerks the car to a stop. Her face is all red. "That's why your neck and head are fucked up! You're negative! That's why you can't find love!"

"Right now, I just want to feel normal," I shout above the wind.

"Normal? What's normal? Stop fucking the schlump and you'll be normal! He makes you do it upside down, from swings, chains. No wonder your head is loose! Honey, feng shui will turn things around for you. You'll meet the man of your dreams."

"Uh-huh."

"I'll set up the appointment," she says, stopping the car in front of my building. "Bunny Blumenthal used Samm Fu. He's a feng shui expert. Two days later, she met Leonard. The rest is history. She's engaged."

FENG SHUI

The doorbell rings. When I open the door, I'm shocked to see that he's this slim, boomer Jewish man of about sixty, with silver curly hair, dressed to the nines in Armani. He walks into my loft as if he's walking on water and carries a smooth leather briefcase.

"I thought you'd be…"

"Chinese? I studied in China for many years," he says in a cranky voice. "My real name is Sanford Goldman. I'm known as Samm Fu."

"Uh-huh."

He frowns and stares at the piles of books and magazines along the edge of my window seats. He squints at the chairs arranged in front of the window.

"Clutter," he peevishly says. "No wonder you can't get a man interested."

"Uh-huh."

"On a scale of one to ten for clutter, you're a two. That's why you're not married and have a swollen head. Sandy told me. No man wants a slob."

"Uh-huh."

"Do you have a glass of water?"

"Sure."

I schlep out my last bottle of good bottled water, and he sniffs it first to make sure it's not dirty or something, and then he drinks it.

Now he stands in the center of my loft, swinging a little steel ball dangling from a thin wire. His eyes are closed, and he's muttering this voodoo shit. When the ball moves, he lets out impatient moans. As he moves from corner to corner, the ball moves faster.

"Which means that there's bad energy here," he says, frowning. "Very bad."

"Oh, my God," I murmur. "I've had—visits."

"The spirits hate it here. They tell me this. They hate the clutter. You have to get rid of all the schmatas!"

"Antiques I inherited—"

"Schmatas!" he shouts, looking disgusted. "Not to mention these paintings! The women don't have heads!"

"I paint women without heads. They don't need their heads—"

He closes his eyes. "Either you want a happy life or paintings of women without heads. They represent a broken spirit."

"Uh-huh."

Then he starts moving furniture around, making a friggin' mess, explaining that the spirits need "space."

By now, my head is hurting big time. Two hours later, he gives me this friggin' bill for five hundred dollars.

"Oh, Sandy said you cost fifty dollars."

"Was she born in the fifteenth century?" he shouts, his face turning red. "Has she heard of inflation? I have a house in Sedona to take care of! Bills! Five hundred is a bargain. You're a successful psychologist, but your place is a mess. I made a diagram showing where you should move your furniture. Or you'll never meet Mr. Right."

"Uh-huh. But I can't move the furniture because of my neck. Now I have to hire someone to move it."

"Bunny Blumenthal said you're a nut case. If you don't pay me right now, I shudder to think of the curse on this house."

Terrified, I agree.

He hands me a red silk and gold brocade tiny purse with red tassels dangling from the bottom. "Fold the check," he instructs. "I can't touch germs. Put the money in the envelope, and then seal the envelope. Do what I say."

"Sure, uh-huh," I say, postdating a check and hoping it won't bounce, then folding it and placing it inside the brocade purse, careful not to touch the edges.

He stands then, and I walk him to the door. He looks at me one more time and says, "I'll pray for you. Remember, a clean house is a clean spirit."

BOOMER HOTTIES

"Bunny Blumenthal gave her new freak fiancée a blowjob and lost her new ten thousand-dollar bridge. "He hasn't called since. Bastard," says Sandy, placing a bowl of organic chicken salad on the buffet.

It's boomer hottie night. We're at Sandy's Victorian house on California Street. I haven't seen the girls for a while, and even though we talk every day, I miss being with them.

Sandy's house is set off a narrow street in North Beach. A small house, but the central kitchen and rooms open to the view of a magnificent English-style garden of tall flowers and colors and trees. After a delicious dinner of Japanese marinated noodles, salad, and chicken, we sit around the fireplace on the sapphire blue velvet couch, and pale apricot silk chairs. On a large, square wood table, terra cotta bowls are filled with seashells Sandy collects, and on a shelf are jade, turquoise, and amber bowls. French songs play from the stereo and a strong wind blows the wind bells dangling from the open windows.

Niki is showing pictures of George on her iPad. He's drop dead gorgeous. For the first time, she's in love.

"I'm playing hard to get. This time, I'm not getting into the confrontation stuff right away, like what are your plans for our future, stuff like that. I can't believe I ever did that. This guy's too good."

"Be a little bitch," I advise. "I don't like the no calling for days after sex."

"Amen," Sandy says, serving coffee in glass cups.

Sandy is dating a chef she met at a food show. "He can cook, but he can't fuck. He has prostate cancer. But we spoon."

"I'll take the spooning over the commitment phobic who gives great sex and no affection," Lorraine says, glaring at me.

"Jeffrey and I are renting a house together!" Nancy announces. "I'm selling my condo."

"Your paid-for condo? Are you crazy?" we all say together. "Why?"

"I need the money." She continues knitting a beautiful, long wool scarf.

"You mean Jeffrey needs the money," Lorraine states angrily. "Big mistake. Big. You'll end up paying more rent, and plus, you rent a huge studio for him. Not good."

"He needs the studio for his performance pieces. Also, he has three children, and I've always wanted a family."

"Buy a dog." Lorraine snaps.

"He'll go through everything," Niki says, a look of concern on her lovely face. "A lot of boomer men only want a successful woman so they can live in her lifestyle. Before he met you, he worked at Kinko's and wore thongs. Who is this guy?"

"Brilliant, he's brilliant," Marcy says defensively. "He had an art fellowship for his performance piece."

"You mean in 1963," Lorraine quips. "I googled him. He sat in a store window for three days, staring. He's a freak."

"He's got you sexually brainwashed," Niki adds.

"That's what happens to a lot of us," I say vehemently. "We women are programmed to think sex is sacred. Ancient Amish stuff. We're like Amish in drag."

"Look at poor Bunny Blumenthal," Sandy continues. "Now she's involved with a fortune hunter who pretends he's wealthy. He hasn't a bean. He went through his dead wife's money, and now he's spending Bunny's money. She has sex with this drip all the time, but her money's running out."

"Women who earn money should keep their money separate—"

"The freaks not only think they can replace their dead wives, but they expect us to pay. No way," Niki says vehemently

"They'll have to steal it to get it from me," I say. "I'm finally making money and it's for Nanny. I'm new school. What's mine is mine and not his. If a man invites me out, or wants my company, he pays."

"Amen."

THE HAIRCUT

I need a makeover. It's funny with glamour. It's something you feel. It doesn't come out of a bottle or with a new pair of expensive shoes; no, glamour is a mirror that reflects how you feel about yourself. Also, I'm booked for lots of speaking engagements about how everything is possible at every age, and I want to look as good as I feel. Marcy told me about this "great stylist," and her hair always looks ready for Vogue. So chic.

I arrive at the salon, a large spacious room with white, high-polish, lacquer walls and Madonna music amplified so loud a headache is kicking in. An assistant about twenty, with purple hair and hostile eyes, leads me to the dressing room, where I change into a black robe with wing-like sleeves and gold stars in the print.

Then another assistant wearing a black H&M top, with black streaks in her gold-dyed hair, and two nose rings, piles a bunch of outdated *People* magazines in my lap and brings me a glass of bottled water with a wrinkled lemon rind floating on the top. All these socialite types, with bobbed silky hair and legs thin as picks, sit around having manis and pedis.

A gorgeous Asian girl with black silky hair flopping to her waist and impersonal eyes introduces herself as, "Waters, your stylist."

"I want my hair long, but shaped. I like it a bit longer in the back, slightly layered on the side."

She lifts my hair, dropping it between her long thin fingers, frowning. "Your hair is thin. It needs to be shorter."

"Not too short," I say. "I want the ends shaped."

"Women your age should not wear long hair if the hair is thin."

"Uh-huh. I can't wear my hair short," I protest.

"Your hair is very thin," she repeats. "It's not good hair. It needs major shaping."

She instructs Jose, a hair intern hovering near Waters, his obsequious eyes on her every move, to shampoo me. He wears a tight black t-shirt, his gorgeous, shiny, black hair spiked up.

"Give her a hot oil treatment," Waters instructs impatiently. "Her hair is like straw."

Jose brings me to a sink. As he shampoos my hair, he pushes my neck back and forth and sighs impatiently.

"My neck. I have arthritis. Do you mind if you don't move my neck so much?"

"If you sit back, it won't hurt," he snaps, drenching my hair with conditioner then spraying my head with hot water, dripping down my back.

Finally, he wraps a towel around my head like a bandage and sullenly leads me to my chair at Water's station.

Like a surgeon ready to operate, Water holds thin scissors. Checking out her elegant image in the tall mirror, she pauses, sighs, then begins cutting.

Snip. Snip. Snip.

"Not too short," I repeat.

Wet curls fall to the floor, like rings. The music is blasting, and while she cuts, she talks into her mouthpiece, having an intimate conversation with someone she calls Raoul. This is what I'm paying three hundred dollars for? Plus, I can't see how much she is cutting because my glasses are off and I'm nearsighted. All I can see is a blur in the mirror.

She finishes cutting, her hands thumping my head around, squinting her eyes at a few loose strands, then snipping again. Then she nods to Jose and instructs him to "blow her out."

He blows my hair with this humongous, heavy blow dryer, pulling clumps of hair so hard my head snaps back. "Sit straight," he orders.

He turns off the blower.

I put on my eyeglasses so I can see. I am horrified. The sides are longer than the back; it's a flapper haircut, good on a very young girl with thick, straight, Asian hair. My very wavy hair looks thinner, and my jowls hang out.

Jose reverently gushes how "glam" my new haircut is. "It's so Cameron Diaz."

"I hate Diaz's hair. She has lousy hair!"

Waters comes over. "You look—*younger*," she gushes reverently.

"I don't want to look younger. I like my age. One side is longer than the other side," I say, my voice rising.

"You looked like a mess when you came in. Now you look like a diva," Jose says snippily. Waters is on the phone again. Jose walks away.

In the dressing room, I quickly dress. Someone stole my Hermes scarf.

Outside, it's raining. I don't cover my hair. The rain curls my hair and the sides are dangling like wet strips of plastic.

At home, I cut the dangling sides to match the back. I decide that the next day I'll go to Super Cuts to even it out.

Depressed about my lousy haircut, I grill my salmon fillet on my George Foreman grill, happily eating and watching the horrible news on television. As I watch ads with perfect-looking models bouncing along meadows with hair that undulates like ripples on a sea, I wonder if we are all about image. My grandmother wore a bun at the back of her hair, and it was down to her waist, until she died. I thought she was glamorous. She felt that way, too.

BLIND DATE

This dating life is exhausting. Still, with each one, I anticipate he'll be it. Meanwhile, I'm trying to finish my sequel, and my patient list has grown. To relax, I spend time walking or at the museums, where I find solace and new questions.

Tonight, I'm going out with Herb Hoffman. Herb looks like Tony Bennett. He has close-cropped silver hair, olive skin, this Godfather aura about him. He's a blind date. The lawyer who lives in my loft building fixed us up. I'm in his silver Mercedes, which smells like new leather, on our way to the restaurant. Herb's a well-known prosecutor, and he's been married five times. "But he's cool," the lawyer friend had said, and he's "looking for a partner." Anyway, he carries two cell phones, an iPad, and a Blackberry. He said he has different numbers on each phone and needs the equipment. "If a client calls, I know which cell phone to answer. If it's personal, my iPhone 5 beeps a programmed sound."

"Wow. It must get confusing."

"Honey, life is complicated. Gotta be prepared."

But I'm trying for a new attitude, and who knows?

At stop signs, he sneaks looks in the rear view mirror, checking me out. Too slick for my taste. But since I'm doing a case study on why men marry multiple times, he might be interesting.

I make small talk about political issues, ranting that the Republicans are bigoted and that I don't believe in incarceration. "It's barbaric! Too many innocent people are deemed guilty."

"Do you want to invite the serial killers to dinner?" he shrieks, jerking the car to a stop at a red light.

"I just meant—"

"Meant what? Meant that you're a communist? What are you? One of those raggy post hippies?"

"No, I—"

The light turns to green. He's driving fast, weaving in and out of lanes, yelling that I sound "nuts," and that he'd googled *Boomer Heat.* "You therapists are out there, honey."

"I just think that our country is sociologically behind in some issues—still fighting over same sex marriage when it should be justice for all, still criminalizing drugs—"

"This is the best country in the world!" he screams louder.

He jolts the car to a stop in North Beach, in front of a restaurant with a green awning. A valet wearing a red jacket and blowing a gold whistle hurries to open the door on my side of the car. Herb, carrying his phones and iPad walks ahead of me, and I'm almost running to follow him into the dark, cave-like restaurant.

The headwaiter greets Herb as if he's royalty, and we're led downstairs to the private wine cellar. Trying not to trip on my brand new, very high heels, I follow them, fighting the impulse to tell this Herb person that I suddenly have a headache.

We're seated and the cellar is so cold, I shiver. Huge vats of wine surround the room, and the air smells of cold wine. Herb makes a big thing about what wine to serve first.

"I would prefer a vodka shot."

He frowns.

"I order a fucking two hundred and fifty-dollar bottle of wine and you want that Russian crap?"

"Wine gives me a headache."

"I don't think we're compatible."

"Hello? When did you figure that out?"

At dinner, he drinks the Sauvignon like water, and I'm on my third vodka shot. He brags about his tennis game, as if he's having a monologue with himself, barely looking at me, the beepers going off on his iPad and phones.

I pick at the dry, wrinkled fish, nodding as he brags about his conquests, travels. "Last week I was in Costa Rica with Nanette. She was my maid, and we got—"

"Involved," I finish. "Why are you with me tonight then?"

He shrugs. "Ace said you were tall and very thin. I'd say you're medium height and—voluptuous." He sighs wistfully. "I'm a sucker for beauty."

"Yes, I can tell," I say sarcastically.

He raps his knuckles on the top of the table.

"Most of the women I take out are twenty-five. They think I'm fifty."

"Do you have something against sixty-eight?"

He shrugs. "I think it's great that you have a profession," he says patronizingly. "Most of the women I meet your age are in assisted living."

"You're an age racist."

"Damn right. There's nothing wonderful about getting old."

"But people in their twenties can be old. Old is a state of mind. How you feel."

"And how you look," he snaps. "Most women your age are covered in hair extensions and fake boobs, but the young ones have skin like silk and give you a run for your money. Women your age are desperate for men. The young girls are romantic—"

"And interested in your money."

"I love spending it. They don't sit here guzzling vodka. They pretend to like the wine, they gush over me."

"Touché."

He glances at his watch. He has to get up early. He has a tennis game at six. Do I mind if he puts me in a taxi?

"No, not at all."

"You're a nice lady. But I'm looking for the right woman."

"I'm sure you'll find her."

At home, I'm in my office writing my case history about Herb. Foghorns bellow like horns.

He's like a ball rolling down a hill, trying to stop. He's afraid of age, death, and is chasing an elusive youth, a dream that he lost somewhere along the line. Something sad about him. Many men stopped developing and can't be more than a provider.

As I write, the sound of the wind bells on my terrace sounds like church chimes, lulling me into my zone. Wind bells. I love the sound of wind bells and the wind on the water. I like this time of night, when it's dead quiet, and I wonder if space sounds like this, or if when you die, if it's quiet, too. Quiet is has its own language and emotions, and words are so noisy.

DID I FORGET TO GROW A NECK?

My neck curls and sags like a purse hanging from my chin. Even my silver Tibetan collar doesn't hide it. Holly Blum had her neck lifted, and now it's part of her lips. What is it with this filler stuff? Why can't we age naturally?

Nathan Craps, an eighty-year-old diamond dealer, went to Brazil for a facelift. His face is as tiny as an olive, and when he lifts his head, you can see the scar from ear to ear. Poor thing. He still has saggy balls and cellulite on his legs. He thinks he looks like George Clooney. God, I've had it with this anti-aging thing, this pressure not to have a sag or wrinkle. Sometimes at night, I can't sleep. I turn on the TV. Nothing on, except reruns of those lipped-up housewives. And I'm sick of seeing Cindy Crawford on those skin commercials, her French doctor za-za-zooming about the melon cells he injects into her flawless skin. Who cares? Get that beauty mark removed from your lip; what makes her think it looks pretty?

Everything has to age. Are we all to be in a wax museum? Is this disparity between our living longer and aging bodies an issue? Do we need to adjust our looks? I don't think good aging is a matter of appearance. Nor do I need to be younger. I am who I am. Your age is who you are.

Skype Me

Norbert Kingman is a sixty- two-year-old widower looking for love. He has a successful hedge fund, and I met him on Boomermatch, a new site for single boomers. He e-mails that he wants to Skype, "get to know each other," he insists, before meeting. I agree.

It's later afternoon. I'm in my office, smoothing my hair and making sure that my office is pristine. Skype is the way of the future. Will save a lot of meetings at Starbucks. Anyway, since I've decided to play the field, it's been exhausting—so many jerks, and at times it feels lonely. But also, I'm getting lots of case histories for the sequel, and soon I will be finished with *Boomer Heat Two*.

I put on my new red Mac lipstick, puff my gold-streaked hair, and then turn on Skype.

"Hello."

"There you are," Norbert says.

His face is so close to the screen I can lick it off. He has this huge face with bulging, goiter-type eyes, and a floppy mane of dark, cranky hair. We make small talk: how long windowed? Kids? Travel? Shit like that. Then, wham, I hear a toilet flush loudly and then these loud pooping sounds.

Oh, my God! He's on the john. Doesn't he know that I can see him taking a dump? His pants dropped and twisted around his ankles, even the hairs on his thick, white fat thighs? He keeps moving his laptop around his lap and obviously, he doesn't understand what is happening.

He talks fast and loud and complains about the "dating scene," and how many "stupid women," there are. He doesn't mind if they're "older," he continues, but he wants "smart, successful, and fit."

"The woman I was in love with looked like Pamela Anderson." He flushes the toilet. It makes a gurgling sound. "She broke up with me because I couldn't sustain an erection."

"Shame."

I'm ready to vomit. He's wiping himself now, the computer sliding down his lap and letting me see his you know what and the mound of hairs curled around it.

"The fucking Viagra gave me a migraine and made me impotent," he continues angrily. "I'm suing Viagra for ten million. Viagra is a conspiracy. The government wants to kill men."

"Wow."

"Anyway, the Pamela Anderson lookalike left me an email that she isn't sexually attracted to me."

"I'm sorry. Hard to imagine."

"If only I'd had ten more inches."

"Well, you could always get a penile implant," I suggest. Flush goes the toilet again.

"Not to mention my semen is diminishing."

"Well, I have to go," I say. "Nice talking to you."

"Let me think about if we have anything in common. You look nice, Doc, but if you don't mind my telling you, you could use some— fillers. Skype magnifies the lines on the face."

"Uh-huh. Sure."

I click off Skype and call Sandy.

116

SLEEP

I can't sleep. Okay, so I had a lousy decaf espresso tonight. So sue me. Now I'm lying awake, my heart beating like it's going to climb out of my chest, and it's four a.m. Shit. I've had it with watching the hair ads and Cindy and her French doctor slobbering over her skin.

How will I die? What will happen on the day I die? Will they find life on Mars? Will humans learn to fly, and will cars be obsolete? I'll miss all the fun.

Every night, in case I die in my sleep, I wear cute t-shirts with long sleeves, as I don't want the coroner to see my flabby arms. I make sure that my pedicures are updated with dark red polish, and I spray Chanel #5 on my pussy and on my bed. Before I'm cremated, they'll take off my clothes, and I don't want to smell. Also, I want a good place in line at the crematorium.

Strands of dawn creep along the ceiling, and the traffic outside is speeding up. I turn on the television again, surfing channels. Rot. All I see, again and again, is Cindy Crawford looking at herself in the mirror and ranting about her melon injections. This friggin skin obsession is enough to make you a zombie. A melon is a melon is a melon. Plus, my IBS acts up when I eat melons.

I turn off the remote and only the sound of static exists. I watch a beam of dawn light tremble along the ceiling, and my eyes close, and I slip into sleep.

I dream that I'm flying. I love to fly. I float above George Clooney's bed. He sleeps on his side, his hands folded under his chin. He looks nice. Long eyelashes, silver in his hair. I drop a feather on his face and move on. I'm on my way to meet Clint Eastwood. And my perfume drifts with the wind.

PART THREE:

CONFLICTS AND CHANGES

STARFUCKS

I'm at Starbucks. Every day, after my last patient, I go to Starbucks and drink a decaf iced cap with nonfat soy on top. This is where I meet my freak blind dates or write up case histories on my iPad. The small cafe is full of dot com refugees working on their Apple laptops, iPads, Kindles, smart phones.

My cell phone rings. It's Nanny. She's hocking about this new singles site that she wants me to go on.

"Nada. Been there, done that."

"You have a rotten attitude!" she shouts.

"Don't shout."

"I'm not shouting!"

"You're shouting!"

Nanny hangs up.

"Hey lady! Keep your voice down," shouts a cranky-looking man with a mohawk.

"Then don't listen," I say. "Go to a library."

"Take your calls outside," he orders.

He wears a T-shirt printed with *Silicon Valley* on the front. He has mean, tiny eyes and a pin head.

"Everyone leaves because of you," chimes a fat girl behind him. She has blonde curly air, and she eats a bag of chips.

"Who asked you to listen?" I snap.

A man around my age, with white, wavy long hair, and dark, smooth skin, defends me. "Everyone talks on the phone," he says gently to the man and woman. "If you want quiet, go."

"Wow, thank you."

He nods formally, but he has shiny blue eyes. "I know how it is. I get calls here, too."

"Katy," I say, extending my hand.

"I know. You're Dr. Katy."

"How do you know?"

"I've seen you around the neighborhood. My office is near here." He pauses. "I've read *Boomer Heat*. I recognized you by the photo on the back of the book."

"Wow. So I'm famous."

He smiles.

"Are you famous?" I ask playfully.

"Somewhat," he says modestly. "Jesse Jankowitz. Nice to meet you, Katy Roseman."

"The director?"

He nods.

"God. I love your last film about Frida Kahlo. It's—compelling."

He nods. "It took nine years to make. I'm glad you liked it."

"You captured the reality of an artist. Not of the patrons. You captured her point of view."

Dimples crease his cheek. "Do you live near here?"

"My loft is two blocks away."

He returns to his computer. The conversation is closed. I resume working on my iPad. His cell phone rings a couple of times, but he

121

turns his head and speaks softly. I can't make out what he's saying. I Google him on my iPad. Married forty-seven years to a writer. She died in 2009. I'm attracted. Disconcerted. Nervous. This man has a special aura.

"Well, see you around," he says, standing.

"I hope so," I say boldly. "Let me give you my card."

He waits politely. I fumble in my huge tote bag and remove a coffee-stained card with my email and cell phone on it. "Found it," I say.

"Okay, Katy Roseman. I'll see you."

I watch him walk to the door. He's tall and very slim, and he doesn't walk like an older man. He walks with purpose and stride. Something about this man moves me. He's the kind of man I fantasize about. Strong. Confident. Kind.

Or is love only a fantasy?

JOSH

At times, I want to dump Josh, and I get really angry at myself for putting up with his deceitful ways. But other times, when he brings old, soggy roses tied by a rubber band and his red tool kit to fix things, my heart flutters. It's so complicated, this sexual attraction thing.

Tonight, past midnight, Josh and I are lying in bed. The radio is on to smooth jazz, and Ella is singing "Summertime." Earlier, we'd been to a movie and then back to my place to make love. The room is dark, and moonlight flows from the open window, dropping circles of light along the tall, white ceiling. We're holding hands, lost in our own thoughts.

"I didn't tell you, Josh. My ophthalmologist says I have cataracts. I have to have surgery."

"It's nothing," he yawns.

"Every minute it's something. Now I have cataracts, IBS, arthritis in the neck. Geez."

"You're beautiful," he says, squeezing my hand.

"Do you think so?" I cuddle next to him.

"Ssshhh. Don't talk. Look at the stars. There's Polaris."

"Where?"

"See that explosion of light radiating in the room? That light is from Polaris, the most radiant of all stars." He holds me tight. "I take you with me to Polaris."

I laugh. "Is Polaris your favorite star?"

He sighs. "You could say that. But there are many trillions of beautiful stars. Not just one star."

"Like women? Is that why you don't want just me?"

"I want just you as you are. As we are."

"On Friday nights. That's not enough."

He sighs again. "If we were to conform to being together all the time, we wouldn't be us. I wouldn't be me. My Friday nights with you are a marriage in itself. Full of love and wonderful things. Just like Polaris radiating its own light."

"But I want an us," I persist. "I want to be with someone who says I love you before we sleep, when we wake, to be together on holidays, in sickness and in health, in joy and sadness. I want it all. I want—Josh, Josh, oh my God, you're sleeping—"

For a long time, I watch the light radiate along the ceiling, then slowly darken in patches, and when it's gone, I sadly know that if I don't end it now, I'll never have what I want.

BREAKUP

"Vodka?"

"Josh, I have something to tell you."

"It's imported from Russia." He pours vodka into our shot glasses. He's at my loft. He's expecting dinner and an overnight.

"Sorry I haven't called," he says with a nonchalant shrug. "Had to go to Stuttgart to deliver a paper."

"Sure, uh-huh. Did Svetlana go with you?"

Josh coughs.

There's a fire in the fireplace, and the flames make a crackling sound, mingling with the sound of rain slamming the windows. Yellow roses fill the vases of my loft. Every three mornings, I go to the flower mart and buy yellow roses.

"I thought tomorrow we'd go to the Man Ray exhibit at the Legion," he says. "Then I have to head back. I'm giving a paper on Jupiter. I have graduate students to see."

"Your Russian is a graduate student."

"Katy, let's not do this."

"Do what?"

"This."

"This is what I don't want anymore."

He sighs.

"This is what I have to tell you, Josh. Go with your planets and stars. Maybe you'll do better in space. I mean it, Josh. I don't want you to call or e-mail me again. I want to end this habit I've had, this delicious and poisonous habit of sex with you on Friday nights. It's not fair that I've been using you for sex."

He laughs, as though I'm making a joke.

"I'm serious. I've put up with your cold deceits so I'd have good sex. I've done what I advise my patients not to do—traded me to get something from *you*. Instead of loving myself, I wanted love from you. I broke my rules, and each time I lost something of myself."

"You're too analytical. I'm not your patient."

"But you are."

"I know I hold you at arm's length. Let's see what happens—if there's going to be anything more—"

"Closeness comes from intimacy, and is not doled out only on your terms. It's been great in some ways, but I want more."

He looks at me, as if he isn't sure whether to believe me or not. He finishes his drink, and slowly, indolently, puts the drink on the metal table. Then he stands, zips his parka, and slowly, indolently, shuffles to the door, not lifting his feet, opens it, and leaves.

When the door slams, I feel for the first time, relief. Know that this time I mean it. Won't settle. It's over, finally. I feel lighter. With each new decision, comes a transition, and with each new transition comes a new choice. The journey is like that—a series of ups, downs, twists, and turns. It's infinite.

Boomer Hotties

"George's daughter is lovely, but George was elusive. He pretended we were just buddies. He didn't show any affection around her."

"Men are so afraid of commitment," I say. "But they want it all."

"Maybe when he gets used to your being with the daughter it will stop," Marcy says, knitting a scarf for her boyfriend.

"Nothing stops unless you see that it does. You have to handle these boomer guys with tender loving care. God forbid they think you want something."

"Look at Bunny. She now finds out her freak so-called fiancée has another woman he's in love with. So her money has been given to his twenty-five-year-old Swedish nanny he met in the park, walking Bunny's poodle. Can you imagine? Poor Bunny. She's having a nervous breakdown. She said he had such a large cock that she's tripped over it. She gave him everything. Dummy."

"How can she be so stupid? She's a smart lady, yet so stupid about men."

"She never got out of her generation where women were supposed to breathe for men. She's terrified of not having a man."

"So many women, brilliant women, with careers and professions like us, are wimpettes for a man. We've all been there."

"Marcy is still doing it," Lorraine says, glaring at Marcy, who concentrates on knitting.

"That isn't very nice," I say.

"If we sisters don't tell each other the truth, then who will?" Niki says. "It's hard enough without the truth."

"Amen."

DR. ARCHIE LAVIN

"Hello. It's Dr. Archie Lavin. We met on Serendipity.com."

"Levin?"

"L A V I N!" he spells impatiently, sighing as though he's irritated.

"Oh, uh-huh, you're the root canal dentist."

We shoot the breeze about on-line dating. He rants about how really "sick," on-line dating is, and how most of the women are rejects.

"The ugly ones show fake photos," he laments. "I don't need to show a photo. If you've got it, you don't need to flaunt it."

"Uh-huh. Great."

"Do you have Comcast?"

"Also, Netflix," I reply.

"Let's meet. Tonight? At Tai on Polk Street."

"Does it have a bar? I like martini shots."

"Yes. And the food is wonderful."

At six o'clock, I'm at Tai. The bar has two wobbly bar stools and only wine and beer. I wish I had my flask. I arrive early. I always arrive early. Abandonment issues.

In walks this man with a Gumby squishy body and a very small head. He has nasty, colorless eyes and a small goatee shaped into a point. When he smiles, his teeth are so white they glow.

"So we meet," I say, wanting to go home.

"You look different than your picture on your column," he says peevishly, frowning at my chandelier earrings.

"Surprise! Surprise!" I laugh.

"You have nice veneers," he says. "You passed the first test. A lot of these older women have faces so tight they can't smile, but they have rotten teeth."

"Uh-huh."

At the table, he studies the menu. "I'll have the number two," he tells the waiter.

"The twelve for me."

Over dinner, he noisily slurps worm-looking noodles into his mouth, yakking about his dead wife.

"Shame."

"She had rotten teeth. I redid her whole mouth. I made a doll out of her."

"Pygmalion."

He shrugs. Then he continues to tell me about their "lousy sex life," how ungrateful she was, and that he'd bought her a house, a sailboat, and Warhol prints, but she always wanted more.

"She spent all my money. Next time, my woman has to have her own money. I'm not a bank!"

"How did she die?" I ask after a while.

"She choked in a Japanese restaurant, eating seaweed. The waiter tried to pull it from her throat, but she gagged, and we couldn't revive her."

"Oh, my god."

"It was embarrassing. There was my wife, vomiting and gagging, her legs spread to Timbuktu, everyone crowded around."

130

I don't reply. How can you reply to this horrible man? Is there any true love? Any loyalty? Or does marriage kill it? Then what about the great loves I read about? Zelda and Scott Fitzgerald, Napoleon and Josephine? Others? But then again Zelda and Scott tormented each other…

"Do you have any money?" He takes a bite from a raisin bun.

"I'm not a nurse with a purse. I have a profession. I find your question insulting."

"Honey, if you haven't made it yet with a partner, what makes you think you'll make it now?"

"My dreams."

"My dream is to have a good piece of ass and some good home cooking. My wife was a rotten cook and always dragged me out. I'm ready for a relationship."

"Yes, I can tell."

So the rest of the dinner he complains about the forty years he lived with his wife Edith. Nastily, he complains that she was "too short. A stump." He continues putting the poor woman down, and telling me that he's ready for "glam."

"I bought my wife a ten thousand-dollar posturepedic bed, the Cloud. Push a button here, there, and bingo, you're in heaven. Wanna try it?"

"No thanks. I'm looking for true, undying love."

He adds up the wrinkled bill with a tiny calculator. "Anyway, I like the Angelina Jolie type."

"Gotcha."

Outside, we stand under the moon.

"Well, good luck on your search for love," he says.

Under the moonlight, I see the sadness etched into the lines on his face. When you don't acknowledge your own soul, know who you are, sadness drowns the soul.

I watch him schlump away.

TELEVISION

Winter is in the air, and frost lies on my windows like lace. I surf the television channels, leading the remote from one channel to another. Nothing. Only those ugly Orange County housewives yelling, bitching, and whining about their help and clothes and ugly husbands. God, I can't stand them. That awful Vicki is always screaming, "Woo Woo!" Who cares? Plus, she dumps her cool husband for this freaky, weird, Southern jerk who gives her pathetic Hallmark greeting cards and a skunky fur coat he probably got off the mafia truck. Plus, he's icky. Tamra, you're a witch. Without your extensions and make up, you look like an apple on a stick. Eddie is moronic, the kind of guy I liked in the seventh grade. Goes to India on a spiritual quest.

Kardashian is definitely a special needs child. She talks like an idiot, a question on the end of each sentence. Get a dictionary—and what's with the clown makeup and the chunky, huge boobs hanging out of everything? She's really awful. I think she should take a training program at PETA. Not to mention the freak men she's with. Okay, I'm mean. I can't help it. The morons that the networks choose to show to the world exacerbate my mean side.

I surf to the hideous celebrity group therapy programs to vomit even more. That dummy, fake-blonde Linda, with black eye shadow, her eyes rimmed like an owl, dumb as a rock, who was married to the

Hulk, cries because her boyfriend (twenty-nine years her junior) was on Facebook giving a look.

Who are these retards? How can we put them on? It's bad enough with the fashion programs—the latest, *Fashion Star*. Oh, my God, all these designers crying if they don't get orders, a bunch of D-list stars pontificating about fashion. And then, what's with *The Bachelor*? Never have I seen such wimpy, stupid girls who, after getting one limp rose, cry on national television that they're in love. Poor things. Plus, the guys are really pathetic. Not to mention the "millionaire matchmaker," Patti Stenger. God help us all. Another babe who screams in your face and gives rules for dating. Where is her spouse? And is she Amish with her outdated, ancient virgin rules? Not to mention her puffy fake lips, boobs, and those assistants with the spiked hideous hair. Oh, my God, are they aliens? Is this what television has succumbed to? The valley of morons?

Okay, the elevator music is rising. The dumbed-down bachelor chooses Muffy, who squeals and rushes to hug him. Tears rush down her Iowa face, swollen from fillers. Ceremoniously, the bachelor gives her a rose, which she presses to her hefty, implanted breasts. The remaining girls, moronic expressions on their heavily made-up faces, cross their fingers; tears rush down their rouged cheeks. Next, he calls Michelle. Several girls look angry, but try to smile. Michelle, a tall, klutzy blonde from Texas, hugs and pats him—you know that hand-patting thing they do when hugging, as if checking out his body, and three times, she "thanks," him. Is this what women have come to? Fighting over one moron, reject guy? What's wrong with women? Then the Bachelor guy takes his time making a decision, and finally, as if he's made an A in potty training, he chooses the six final contestants.

The host of the show instructs the remaining girls to "say their good-byes to the bachelor," while the six winners are high-fiving and congratulating each other, as if they won the Lotto. The remaining girls are instructed to "say good-bye" to Mr. Perfect. The camera follows their grief to the limo that waits to bring them home, their dreams of marriage and fame dissolved.

Archie Bunker and Edith hold up. Lucy and Desi. Great writing, and real issues and real family values.

Then there's the news and political panels. Enough to make you vomit. Pierce Morgan—nice guy, but he talks so much I scream, "You asked him a question, then don't answer it! Let your guest talk! Stop pressing your mouth! You look insipid, not inspired!"

Now a gaunt reporter with an anorexic face in a monotone reports that ten gang members were murdered. "Shot and killed!" she lisps.

"So stop the guns!" I shout. "Do something! Help these kids! Worse, these Tea Party babes come on now, in nasal, tight voices, reciting the gun laws. Especially Miss icky-hair lady, Ann Coulter, who makes a career of trashing President Clinton, our greatest president, for a blowjob by a fat Jewish girl. She's a racist, talks as if she has mush in her mouth, tossing her blonde mane, like a horse. She's the Queen Bee of the Klux Klux Klan, and she found a niche of hate, and people buy it. Geez.

Not to mention Tabatha. She's cute. But who cares about dirty hair salons and out-to-lunch hairdressers? Not important. Another geez. Whoops. There go the chef shows, chefs standing at attention, their eyes full of tears while the foodie gulps their food then whines that the poor chef's hard earned dish "lacks" salt or some damn thing. What's with the mean shit on television? And we wonder why kids bully other kids in the schools. It's a bully nation.

Whoops. Breaking news. An elephant got loose. No wonder. Elephants are angry. They should be tied up in a circus. Another shooting. Now the Tea Party panels are defending the "Constitution."

I've had it.

BEBE

As usual, Bebe looks great. She's sixty-four, has this tight little worked-out body, a sassy attitude, and a thick Jersey accent. She's an editor for a dot com company, but recently lost her job. She's married a long time to a landscape architect, but is bored. She has smooth olive skin, green eyes almost hidden under a huge fringe of bangs, and chin-length, curly brown hair. She wears a tight, little, black leather jacket with silver zippers, really cool, tight jeans, and humongous high heels with straps that wind around her ankles, like snakes.

We're drinking papaya martinis, complaining about the men in our generation. Bebe spends most of her time working out in the gym. She complains that her husband can't get it up and she's having an affair with her electrician.

"Wow."

"I love my husband, but I miss sex. I like sex. Edwardo has a body that won't quit. A great butt and penis. He's dumb as a rock, but who cares?"

"Is it great?"

"It's perfect," she says, wistfully. "But he's too stupid. I need someone I can have pillow talk with. So I joined Sexual Partners for Married People.Com, a social network for men who are also married but want good sex."

"Well, long as your husband doesn't know. Gotta do what you gotta do."

"Amen," she says. "Trick is not to have anyone hurt. Anyhoo, I've met a bunch of freaks. One's uglier than the next, but they're all charged up for sex."

"Wow."

"The last one I met sounded promising. His resume profile was great. You know, Harvard MBA, handsome headshot. We Facetime, and he's all face. Really hot. So we meet at this out-of-the-way bar—you know they're terrified they're going to get caught—so there's all these codes and secret passwords. Turns out, he's four feet tall, all head, with this tiny body."

"Oh, my God."

"The next one I meet is dumb as a skunk. He demands to know right away if I like top or bottom."

"Oooh."

"Poor thing had splayed feet and is a little person. His wife was cheating on him. But this guy hung upside down to please you. Orgasmic sex like I've never had. Upside down, backwards, doggie, duck, fuck, you name it. Even water sports."

I'm laughing my head off, and we're drinking like sluts. But her stories make me sad. Is sex the most important thing? What about intimacy and affection? Or am I old-fashioned?

Outside, we hug goodbye. We promise to get together soon. "To be continued," Bebe says, rushing into the street to get a taxi.

I walk the rest of the way home, my eyes on the moon. Yes, I'm sure there's a man in it. Anyone can see it. He's there.

PET PEEVES

I have many, but I especially detest the way the little plastic caps are placed on medication bottles. Don't the inventor morons know that when you place the bottle on the shelf it's top heavy and topples over, and if the top is loose, the pills spill into the toilet bowl, or sink, or floor? That you have to have twenty-twenty vision and be a rocket scientist to figure out which arrow to turn and how to open it? What happened to the old turn-bottle caps, or even the rubber pop-up ones?

BONE DENSITY

I'm shrinking. I know I'm shrinking because I made a black dot on the wall and now my head is below it. My head looks too large for my shrinking neck. My neck hangs like a purse. I order anti-age shit from the Internet, but then I don't get the products, and they keep the money. At five-feet-eight, I was always the tall girl; I wore flats and slouched so I wouldn't be taller than the boys. I never thought I was shrinking, until recently I noticed that next to my five-foot-nine daughters, I feel like a Lilliputian.

"Time for a bone density test," my doctor says.

It's Thursday afternoon, a freezing day, fog floating over San Francisco like a soft coat. I'm in the damp hospital basement, sitting on a cold, wooden bench, waiting my turn for the bone density x-ray. Have they heard of a heater? Shivering, I'm wearing this lousy blue cotton gown with tiny orange ants printed on it, leather clogs, and black knee socks, my pale veiny legs sticking out. Not to mention I'm having a bad hair day, my thin ponytail tied with a nebbish black scrunchy. Plus, next to me sits this great-looking boomer hunk, I'd say in his seventies—Semitic Jewish face, a puff of loopy salt and pepper hair, smooth, dark olive skin. He's reading the arts section of the *New York Times*. I take off my coke-bottle-thick glasses and say, "Don't you just admire De Kooning's sensual line? It's so—"

140

"Dreck," he sullenly shrugs. "My wife was a better painter."

"Wow."

"That was before she ran off with the kid who trimmed our lousy grass. Served her right to die."

"Anyway, I'm Katy," I say.

"Dr. Duke Edelman."

"What kind of doctor?"

"I'm a dermatologist."

"Wow. Pimples and lines and Botox?"

He shrugs.

Then he starts telling me how he's working on new laser treatments for the skin, and that he's a vegan and an atheist.

"Atheists are interesting," I say. "Better than the Tea Party."

He glances at his watch. He brags that his doctor told him that he has the bones of a thirty-five-year-old. "Why in hell am I here? I'm a marathon runner. I run with thirty-year-old Russian women, and they can't keep up with me."

"Wow, good bones."

"Bones are important," he says.

"Bones, yes," I say.

"No offense, but you're in your sixties?"

"Proud of it."

He purses his lips. "You look pretty good, though you could use laser. Your skin is a dead giveaway. Most of the women your age have humps in their backs, brittle bones. The last one I made love to cracked her back. She's in a body cast. They don't have the bones."

His name is called, and I watch him

FROG PRINCE

*H*e calls himself the Frog Prince. He's a famous matchmaker in the bay area. He'd read my book on boomers, called, and we agreed to meet at a café on Union Street. He said he'd be reading a book on Obama.

I arrive at the cafe. It is a fog-spilled day. Tourist buses rattle along the narrow streets, past rows of expensive shops and restaurants. I stand by the door then I see a short, squat man reading a book on Obama. A laptop computer is in front of him, next to a Kindle, an iPad, and two phones. He wears a cap, *Frog Prince* printed on the green visor.

At the table, I announce that I'm Katy Roseman.

He closes the book, his emotional brown eyes intently on my face. "I knew you'd be beautiful."

I smile and sit next to him.

We talk a while, mostly about his matchmaking business.

"Why frogs?"

"You have to kiss a lot of frogs before you find the prince. I'm the prince."

"I see."

"Most couples end up in divorce," he says gloomily. "As a therapist you know that relationships are on the line. Technology has taken over."

So while he laments that soon robots will take over and that "robotic therapy" will be the profession of the future, about how hard it to have a relationship, I sip the organic tea he ordered and chew on the organic raisin cookie.

"Do you have family money?" he asks impatiently.

"Is this an audition?"

He shrugs. "You're uptight."

"I believe in serendipity."

Then the frog prince yaks about the positive aspects of smoking grass. He confides that his last wife jumped off the Golden Gate Bridge and that their son is in a mental institution. He's very sad.

"My God, I'm sorry."

"Ten minutes after she died, they dragged her body to the bridge, and Anderson Cooper covered her suicide on CNN."

"My God."

"You're godding."

"I don't know what to say."

"I think you do. You want to say Frog Prince isn't for me."

I sip the tea.

"I'm a frustrated writer. But the world doesn't know dreck from genius. All they know is reality TV and rap songs with lyrics like *Fuck the police, kill the bitch.*"

I glance at my watch. "I'm afraid I have to go. I have a patient in an hour—"

So what do you think?"

"About what?"

About us."

143

"What about us?" I ask.

"Well, you either have chemistry or you don't," he snaps impatiently.

"I just don't want what you want. But I like you, Frog Prince."

"Say, you've gotta come to the Frog Prince Hop. Bring your single friends."

"Maybe I will. Maybe I'll kiss more frogs."

ON THE PHONE WITH NANNY

"Now it's the Frog Prince Hop. What next?" Nanny shouts. "Can't you meet, marry, and be happy?"

"You have to kiss a lot of frogs before you meet the prince."

"Hogwash. Just settle on one."

"On who? Those mentals I meet?" I shout. "I don't need to. I have a career, and I'm expanding it! Plus, I'm happy!"

She sighs heavily.

"I don't want a boyfriend. I want a great love."

"A boyfriend is fine. You won't have to go to the Japanese restaurant alone."

"I like eating alone. I like being alone."

She sighs heavily. "Mom, you need to meet the one before you leave the planet. Look at me. I met Harry on JDate.com."

"It took him nine years to propose," I remind her.

"Don't shout!"

"I'm not shouting!" I reply. "It's my ear."

"Get a hearing aid!"

Beeep.

"Hi, honey, it's Sandy."

"I'm on the phone with Nanny, but will you go with me to the Frog Prince Hop, a singles event, tomorrow night?"

"Sure."

"Talk tomorrow."

"Nanny, I'm back."

But the line is dead.

The holidays arrive. It's Christmas. I love this time of year, love the anticipation in the air, the feeling that something new is about to happen. Even the crankiest people are nice. San Francisco is lit up for the holidays, and there's a frost in the air. At night, a cold fog blows over the city like a long, gray coat. So beautiful.

I spend the holidays with Nanny and her husband, and then New Year's Eve with Sandy. We order take-out sushi and watch old movies at my loft. Happiness comes in moments, quiet moments, when your soul is at rest. It doesn't come in the big, frantic moments, or even the highs; it's between, when there's quiet and reflection.

Then my agent calls and says that she's made a "huge deal with a major studio." She wants me in Los Angeles the next day to meet the writers and talk. "I want a house in the Hamptons," she says. "Let's close a deal."

THE MEETING

"Happy, yes."

"They want happy," my agent persists. "You know, love forever happy."

"We have a meeting today with Ricardo Zuckerman, a major writer."

"But he's in his early thirties. What does he know? My men and women are over fifty—"

"Don't argue," says the agent, applying lip-gloss then answering her cell phone. I'm in Los Angeles in her office. It's hot in Los Angeles. It's always hot in Los Angeles. Her office is air conditioned; actually, it's cold. I'm glad I'm wearing my black Eileen Fisher poncho. My agent is on the phone. She's skinny, maybe anorexic, and her face is full of filler. Puffy. Maybe she's in her early fifties, and she speaks with a touch of a don't-fuck-with-me New Jersey accent. She hangs up the phone, glaring at me. "Let's get the show on the road. Trust me."

I sip the cold coffee. My IBS is acting up. I know the signs—a wavy feeling in the stomach, and then—oh, no, it can't happen. I hold my breath.

"Ricardo wants to meet you."

"Sure."

Ricardo's office is white and chrome, and the glare is so white that I have to keep on my dark glasses. He's about forty-five. Reluctantly, he rises from his steel ergonomic chair, stretching his neck forward. He is thin, wears couture snug jeans, and his silver hair is cut Frank Sinatra-style.

"I have a bulge in my spine," he explains, as if to no one. "The ortho tells me if I don't sit with spine ergonomics, I'll be a hunchback, like those women with the dowager's hump."

"Oh, Ricardo, you're gorgeous," gushes my agent.

He glances at his reflection in the mirrored wall facing him. Then, as if seeing me for the first time, he says, "*Boomer Heat* is a miracle. Those poor bastards you write about are fucked up. We need to soften them. They won't make a box office hit."

"*Seven Flew over the Cuckoo's Nest* did," I say. "I won't do television or a reality show. My material needs movie drama."

"So why are you taking up my time?" he screams. "I'm a busy man!"

"Hey, calm down," says my agent. "Katy doesn't mean to argue with you. She doesn't know—"

"The studios don't want after sixty," he snaps, wiggling his neck. He holds his hands flat on the table as if pushing some kind of ergonomic exercise, half-closing his eyes in exasperation. "I have lined up stars to play the therapist on a Lifetime movie. Very glam. Fifty or so—"

"Well, that's not what I had in mind. No offense. I need to think about all this."

"Think? You don't think in this business!" he shouts, glaring at me. "You think gratitude! Time is money."

"Katy just has to take it in. You're a genius, Ricardo. We'll talk it over and get back to you."

"What do you think this is? The valley of the dolls? It's the valley of the trolls. How dare you think?"

"Uh-huh, sure," I say. "I don't want my characters aged down."

"Don't think too long," Ricardo warns.

My agent does this blowing kisses through her fingers, then patting her heart as if he's God or something.

At the end of the day, on the way home, I make the decision to forget Hollywood. It isn't for this project. I'm disappointed, but happy that the book is doing so well and that I made the decision. It's all a learning curve.

Boomer Hypochondriac

I continue to pursue my case histories, always hoping that someday I'll turn and the love of my life will be there. Or maybe I'll be on an airplane, and for once not sitting next to a nun or obese woman or screaming children. Maybe I'll jut turn around, and our eyes will catch, and whammy, that's it. Maybe it's the dream that matters, not the outcome.

Tonight, I'm out with Jeremy Kellerman, a sixty-three-year-old, never-been-married entrepreneur. He's cool. I met him at a fundraiser for African children. In the martini line, we'd started talking about how much we resented Tea Party politics and loved Obama.

Anyway, we're at this healthy, organic, raw vegetable restaurant. Philip Glass music plays from the speakers, and the waiters are real thin and keep asking if everything is all right. I'm starving and dying for pasta or a BLT. Instead, I'm eating this squash thing that's giving me cramps. My date doesn't eat meat. The man's a case—he worries about age, death, the flu, and food poisoning. He has to eat early, so the sun is still out. If he doesn't, he gets a "buzzing," in his head. It's barely six p.m., so the chic chrome and steel restaurant is empty.

Jeremy carefully lays nine pills in a row on the table. He sets the timer on his huge, underwater, steel wristwatch, explaining exactly what each pill is for: water retention, anti-depressants-allergy, diuretics, bones, heart valves, and cholesterol. He has a bone density test once a month. He feels like he's thirty.

"Good for you," I say.

The waiter diligently recites a list of specials, all organic and made by a famous Chef Heinrich. I order pasta, dying for a vodka shot.

He frowns and looks reflective. After much pause, he orders, "Cucumber salad without oil and lemon on the side. No oil on the vegetables. Make sure the lettuce is organic. Make sure the water is bottled. I don't want bacteria in the water."

"Yes, sir. All our vegetables are organic."

"Send Chef Heinrich over. I have questions."

Immediately, this nasty-looking chef with an under bite and a red face comes to the table.

For at least twenty minutes, Jeremy discusses in what "regions," in Italy the olive oil is made. The chef, looking irritated, assures Jeremy that the olive oils are made in Tuscany. "We only use the purest," he assures Jeremy, still frowning.

"You're sure it's not made in Turkey? I don't want food poisoning."

After the exhausted-looking chef returns to the kitchen and Jeremy is finally satisfied, we eat.

Over our salads, we talk about our work. He is "depressed," about his retirement. He loves his work. I want to study acting, perform a one-woman show, get my age march off the ground.

He nods, chewing slowly. He has a bump on his spine and a swallowing problem, and he's afraid of death. I'm the first woman over forty he has taken out in years.

When the main course comes, he looks at his pasta with a suspicious look. Then, as if he's about to perform communion, he eats. Between careful bites, he lectures that it's very important to eat slowly. "If you eat only a little bit," he repeats, "you'll live longer."

"I want to enjoy life and not worry about it."

"When you're dead, you won't know the difference," he replies, pushing his half-full plate aside.

He has a coughing jag. His grandmother died coughing in a restaurant. He's gagging. Several waiters come over and slam him on his back. Finally, he stops. His face is red. Did I know that there's a certain way to swallow? He points to his throat. He gags again. Drinks water. Then he resumes eating. He is sure that the terrorists have poisoned our food. "The government knows this, but they're lazy."

"You sound bleak."

"Sweetheart, it is."

He calls the waiter over. He needs to look at the bottle of olive oil and check the ingredients. "Something tastes funny." The poor waiter brings a bottle of olive oil to the table.

After he takes out his magnifying glass and reads the ingredients, he glances at his watch. He has to hurry. He needs to get twelve hours a night sleep.

"I'm going to fast for four days, and then I'm going to my retreat in Carmel."

"Uh-huh."

"You're a blast."

"You too," I lie.

I'll Stay Only A Few Days

"I'll be in San Francisco. I'll stay only a few days. I can't wait to see you," Maxine, my old friend, says. She lives in Washington, DC, and is a sixty-one-year-old, drop-dead gorgeous widow and sculptor. "We'll go to galleries; I'll take you to dinner. It'll be fun. It's been fifteen years."

"Fun," I say, remembering when Maxine and I were at art school together. How difficult she was, but friends are important, I quickly assure myself.

"I have one bedroom," I tell her. "But you can have my bed, and I'll sleep on the couch in my office. Also, I need to see patients."

"Not to worry. I'm bringing only a few things. Can you believe we're pushing seventy? We'll talk, talk, and talk."

"Uh-huh," I say, thinking she's always been interesting, and for sure, we'll have lots to talk about.

Thursday arrives. I put on my best jeans, tie my hair in a ponytail, and make room in my closet. Debbie always was a clotheshorse. Up to the minute in style.

The doorbell rings. I rush outside to the taxi. There she is, looking chic as ever—porcelain skin, jet black silver-streaked hair cut in a perfect blunt cut to her chin, and wearing a black Italian couture pants suit and a double strand of pearls around her long, thin neck.

We hug and cry and gurgle that seeing each other is like a "minute ago," and what best friends we always were. We don't dare mention that we had a terrible fight and ended up not speaking the past several years.

"You look fabulous," I repeat. "So chic."

"So do you," she says, her black eyes scanning my leggings and long H&M black sweater. "But we must get that hair shaped," she says, her long, ringed hand lifting a strand, eyeing it, and then dropping it.

"I like it. It's finally growing out."

She sighs heavily. She gives me her luggage. "I have arthritis. The doctor said I can't lift anything."

I schlep her two Vuitton bags up the long flight of stairs and she, carrying the smaller bag, murmurs that her "arthritis," is bothering her and that she can't do any "lifting." She is wearing four-inch-high Jimmy Choo shoes.

"Here we are," I say, opening the door and leading her into my apartment.

She stands in the doorway, her very red lips pressed tight and frowning. "A real loft. Like I worked in when I was an art student in Paris."

"Really?"

"Even the movie posters of Audrey Hepburn and Clint Eastwood are so—juvenile. Fresh."

"Uh-huh."

She proceeds to unpack several gorgeous couture suits and dresses in plastic bags and hangs them in my closet, pushing aside my few clothes. Her Chanel makeup and bottles take up my entire master bathroom, and she's even brought her own Chanel towels with the C crest and pushed my Bed, Bath, and Beyond towels on top of the laundry hamper.

Over coffee, we sit on my sofa, talking. She tells me about her former husband Walter. That he left her nothing. "He was a mafia guy. A scoundrel."

"Shame. But you always lived so beautifully."

"On money he embezzled and stole," she continues in her gravely cigarette voice. She lights another cigarette, and I'm getting a headache.

"I don't smoke. If you don't mind."

"Darling, don't be one of those aging yenta bores."

"No, of course not," I cough.

"Let's order Chinese and watch the Iris Murdoch film," I suggest, feeling already exhausted.

She looks horrified. She doesn't eat "like that." Nor should I. "Salt," she repeats several times, her long, ringed hand over her heart. She wants to "dine," at "Fleur de Lys." She's paying.

"It's a fortune."

"Honey, dear, Learn to live like a lady. You've earned it."

"Sure."

"Get dressed."

"Sure."

So she goes into my bathroom and hogs it for another hour. I hear her talking, and I think she's on the phone, but I notice her iPhone on the coffee table. Then she emerges like a goddess through a cloud. She's wearing a chic black dress with long, cutout sleeves and ropes of real pearls. Her makeup is flawless. I change into a black pants suit and earrings to my shoulders.

She looks at me with an exasperated sigh. "I'll buy you some clothes."

"I like this."

"What's there to like? You need couture, real couture. We'll go shopping."

"I'll call a taxi."

At the posh, plush restaurant, she gets out of the taxi and floats ahead, while I fumble in my purse for cash.

In bad French, Debbie orders all these high-end wines and salmon and caviar, pontificating that it's important to live "like a lady," and not a teenager. We talk about her travels, politics, and contemporary art. She then goes on about her need to find a new husband, that Wally her dead husband gave her "diamonds and emeralds and furs, but everything he gave her was "hot," so she has to hide everything. Also, she has to hide her "fortune," in Switzerland.

"Well, you'll meet someone," I say, aware of the sudden tears in her eyes.

She shrugs her frail shoulders. She talks about her dating life with sixty-plus widowers. How depressing she finds it. "These Jewish men aren't sports. I'm not an early-bird girl. I'm a lady used to an expensive lifestyle. A woman like me has to live, learn, enjoy."

"Certainly, yes," I smile.

The bill arrives on a sterling tray. It sits. Sits for a long time. Sits until the waiter comes back and then back again.

156

"Well, it was a wonderful dinner," I say.

She waves her dainty hand, then yawns. "When you visit, I'll reciprocate."

"Reciprocate?"

She nods. "I changed purses and forgot my wallet. Anyway, I have to teach you to live. Look at me! I learn, look, live. I don't quibble over a bill."

"Wow. Get it, yes."

I pay the three hundred dollar bill, assuring myself that of course she'll pay me back.

The following three days she drags me to museums, art galleries, and five-star restaurants. At each place, she realizes that she brought the "wrong credit card," or "changed purses," and I pay for everything. She stays up all night smoking, watching foreign films and talking to herself so loud that I can't sleep. When my patients arrive, she sits in the main room smoking. I'm exhausted, and the smoke bothers me. All night I'm coughing and wheezing while she instructs me to "travel, learn, live."

"Please, don't smoke," I tell her. "I have a migraine."

"You're too *fearful*. You have to *live*," she replies, stretching out "live."

Finally, it's the last day. Maxine insists her "arthritis" is acting up, and she can't "lift a thing." So I once again carry her luggage outside to the limo she called. "Ladies don't take taxis. They have drivers and limos." She wears this dazzling Versace cape, with leopard print satin lining.

"Sure, uh-huh."

She gives me her silver ring set with amber.

"I'll wear it always," I say, slipping it on my pinky finger. We hug. We cry. We promise to go on a Crystal Cruise together, and definitely, every Sunday, we will call. What fun we had, we gush. She gets into the limo.

"Katy, pay the driver, would you, darling? I forgot my cash."

I pay the driver a hundred dollars, and then as the limo drives away, we wave and blow kisses until the shiny black limo disappears into traffic.

SUNDAY MORNING

"Hello," I answer sleepily.

"Did I wake you? It's Sandy."

"No…well, it's okay. I overslept."

"I have something I want to share with you.

"Shoot."

"Last night…well, you know that Lindsay dude, the twenty-eight-year-old South African, English accent, dresses real well?"

"Oh, yes, yes, the guy you met at the market."

"Yes, Mr. Adorable."

"Well, oh, uh-huh."

"Well, last night he came over, and we watched two films on my VCR, ordered an anchovy pizza and then, well, man, we're really attracted to each other. I mean, well, we got it on, I mean…"

"Go on."

"I don't know whether it was in my mouth, my ass, or my eyes. I drank so much. The guy goes all night. Plus, I found out his wife died two weeks ago in his bed. He sobbed all night about how he 'needed to fuck.' So what am I?"

"A crematorium! He dumped her ashes in you! Get rid of the freak." I shout.

"I've had it—"

"Stop giving it up to these shallow dates. Women are better than this. Let's concentrate on good work, and on ourselves."

"Well, how else am I going to meet the one? Go on that drip yenta Patti Stenger's matchmaking show? Meet more freaks? No thank you! You win some, you lose some."

"Okay, I get it," I say, sighing and yawning. "Forget about your vagina and concentrate on your soul for a while. Keep your eyes on the star."

Beeep.

"So anyway, let's all meet tomorrow at Joe's."

PART FOUR:

KATY FINDS IT ALL

CATARACT SURGERY

*I*t's dawn. I call a taxi. Plus, it's raining like hell, forming huge puddles along the San Francisco hills. The driver turns out to be a whacko—he's on the phone and speaking some weird language and driving like a maniac. As if I'm not nervous enough. He arrives at the clinic, and after I pay him, I go inside.

I spell my name six times for an out-to-lunch receptionist who can barely speak English, then get a pile of shit papers on a clipboard to fill out. Geez, every minute with the papers. I sit on this Ikea, wobbly shit chair in the over-crowded, smelly waiting room. One lady is reciting her rosary, and others are slowly turning pages of outdated magazines with the poor Colorado killer on the cover. Nurses and doctors wearing green uniforms and masks covering their faces, run in and out.

All my life I've been nearsighted, was called Mrs. Magoo. Unless I wear my glasses so thick there are circles in them, I can't see. I don't see myself and imagine my face is still as smooth as when I was sixteen. Plus, when I give blowjobs, no way do I want to be up close and personal and see.

Finally, this baby-faced, sour-looking nurse crooks her finger and says, "Follow me."

She leads me into a huge room with people lying on gurneys, some ready to go to surgery, some still sleeping. She pulls the curtain. "You can leave on your clothes; put your shoes and things in the plastic bag."

162

"Sure."

"Give me your arm."

"Sure."

"Christ, I can't find a vein," she frowns. "You have small veins."

"Sorry."

She sighs and pokes around, muttering under her breath until she jams this needle in my hand.

"This is where the doctor will inject you, put you to sleep."

"Great."

She swishes away. I lie here, zoning out. I'm wheeled into a room with strong lights. My ophthalmologist, this hot-looking African American dude, says hello, not to worry, and to count backwards. Then, in what seems like a New York minute, I see tons of stars in my eyes, like silver crinkles, and wham, bam; I'm back in the room with the curtain.

The nurse with the pilly face brings me a paper to read when I get home and hurries me out. As I walk, I notice that I can see clearly. Wow, never did I see like this before; I see street signs and people's faces. I glance in the mirror in the reception room and am shocked to see the lines in my face and bags under my eyes. I had always imagined they weren't there.

At home, I fall asleep, and my dream is in Technicolor, where I'm flying and my arms are rotating in the air, and it's clear as a bell.

When I wake, I'm expecting to see the TV without my glasses, but it's blurry. Shit. Nancy Klein said she saw perfectly right away. Well, maybe it will take a day.

The next morning, I awake and I can't see anything, so I get a taxi to the doctor.

He takes one look into my eye and frowns. "Didn't you take use your drops?"

"Drops?"

"Didn't you read the paper? With the prescription?"

"I didn't see the prescription."

"I'll have to drain the fluid in your cornea. Sit back."

The next thing he has this humongous long needle.

"Don't make a move," he says. And pow, he drains the fluid.

"Now you'll see. But take these drops as described on the prescription. I'll see you next week."

I'm at home now. I'm on the phone with Sandy. "So if it isn't the cataract, it's the hemorrhoid or the shit I've had it."

"Honey be glad you're alive. Most of the boomer freaks have eye transplants, heart transplants, hair transplants. Look at poor Bunny Blumenthal. Finally, she has a new lover, and what does he do before he goes to bed? You got it. He takes out his eyes and puts them in a dish. If it isn't the teeth, it's the eyes. Oh, fuck. Gotta take this call. It's Morton."

DROP

What is it with dropping things? Every minute, I drop something, and then it disappears.

I'm getting ready for the day. Today, I have back-to-back patients. I'm in my bathroom, my coffee beside me, the radio on to Bach. The music brings me to a new place. Every morning, I have a routine for getting ready for the day. I like routine. It's comforting. It grounds me.

After I rinse my face, I slap on the new Olay anti-age crème, until my pale skin shines. Next, I put drops in my eyes, holding my head back so that the drops don't slip down my face. The music is rising, the water running. Now I take my Walgreen multi-vitamins with iron and an aspirin. I try to open the bottle of Lipitor. I take forty milligrams. I hate these friggin' caps on the bottles. What moron thought of these? First of all, they're top heavy, then what's with the *turn to the right, left, press on the arrow*?

Who can see? Some people have cataracts. Don't they get it? Can't they use a normal flip up cap? Dummies. They think if you're over fifty, you need locks on your doors and impossible tops on bottles.

Now I'm in a bad mood. I press my thumb hard on the top. The bottle drops from my hand, and the friggin' pills fly all over the floor.

I'm on my knees. My hand slides along the bathroom tile, picking up nothing but dust and hairballs. Where are the pills? The bottle? "Damn!" I shout to no one. "I heard you drop. Where are you?"

Time is wasting. I finish blow-drying my hair. Now, the ring. I can't work without wearing my good luck amber and silver ring. But the ring drops. I hear it bounce on the floor. On my knees, my glasses on, I look, but no ring. No Lipitor pills or bottle. Nothing but a few paper clips and one red button.

I'm anxious. I'm an anxious person. I like to be on time. Maybe because I have abandonment issues. It's enough that I dropped the TV remote a week ago, and the television has been on all week to CNN. Who can see the buttons on the fancy TV that my son-in-law gave me? He also gave me a robot named Harry. He thinks it will keep me company. This stupid little metal robot stands in the corner. I don't like him.

I get a flashlight, shining it along the floor.

"They couldn't fly away," I say to my daughter Nanny on the phone.

"Mom," she says in a baby voice. "Maybe you should talk to the doctor. You've been losing and dropping things."

"I have not!"

"You lost your cell phone again. You can't find the remote, and then your house keys. Mom—poor thing. This isn't good."

"So what are you going to do? Drop me in a nursing home and put a balloon around my wrist?"

"Don't shout, Mom. Don't get excited. That's why you drop things. Focus."

"I do focus."

"You drop."

"Dropping isn't a disease."

"Don't shout."

"I'm not shouting."

"Focus, Mom. Gotta go."

I look one more time, crawling about the apartment, looking for my dropped keys, glasses, cell phones, credit cards, eyeliners, papers with telephone numbers written on them, all the things that live in some invisible hole. Someday, I'll find the hole. Meanwhile, I have to figure out how to turn off CNN.

Boomer Crank

I'm meeting another blind date. My Aunt Zoe had him call me. His name is Barry Miles. He's a hotshot environmental lawyer who's into film. So he invites me to the Jewish film festival, and I agree to meet him in front of the box office.

When I arrive, the line is already gone and the documentary has begun. I stand by the box office, furious that he's late—hate late—when suddenly, a tall, hulking man with pale, tan, huge hair and a long tan trench coat hurries towards me.

"Hello." I extend a hand.

"We're late," he frowns, his cranky tan eyes narrowed.

"I was here early."

"Let's go. We don't have time for chit chat."

"Sure."

He walks ahead of me, and I follow him into the now-dark movie theater, so dark I'm holding on to the back of his long trench coat. Finally, we're squished in the middle of a row, and everyone is hissing for us to sit down.

He unwraps a candy bar, not even asking if I want a bite. He breathes like a horse, and for the next two hours, he's absorbed into the documentary about the Holocaust .

When the movie is over, everyone is stepping over us to get out, but he sits and is still frowning.

"Well, shall we go?"

"I want to see the credits. Shoosh!" he says.

So we sit through the rest of the credits, rolling down the screen in German, and when the lights go on, as if at a gravesite, frowning, he still sits. Finally, I stand, then reluctantly, he follows as I leave the aisle.

Outside, it's raining cats and dogs and the village is pitch dark. Not a streetlight in sight. I parked in the lot, and he parked a mile away. But he's hungry, he announces, as though I'm not present. He wants to go something to eat. So we walk along the bumpy, isolated street, until we find a half-lit cafe. Inside, a tired-looking waiter is sweeping floors, and the restaurant smells of Clorox. We sit at a wobbly table, and he studies the menu as though we're at the Ritz.

"It's really raining hard," I say, after a long silence.

He closes the menu. "I'm ordering lasagna and a salad."

He doesn't ask if I want anything. I order a bowl of vegetable soup.

"So you practice environmental law," I say after a rude silence.

He shrugs and looks at his watch.

"Al Gore was right," I persist. "The planet is burning up."

"Al Gore is a moron. He doesn't know anything about ecology, treaties."

He presses his lips and then checks his iPhone for text. You rude bastard, I want to say. Then our food comes, and he's scarfing up his lasagna, not even offering me a bite. The vegetable soup is watery, with a few pale carrots floating on top. Then he starts ranting about his five wives, how really "expensive" marriages are, and that he's a great lawyer, but because of his "bitch wives" and his "generosity," he's broke.

"Shame."

"The last wife broke my heart," he says wistfully. "She was twenty-five. She won the bronze for rowing."

"Wow."

"She ran off with my dog and my guitar and my money."

"But life is full of surprises. So much can still happen—"

"Hey! Are you one of those spiritual do-gooders? This world is fucked. It doesn't have room for love. Don't you know that the world is going to end soon, that the government is in conspiracy with other forces."

"I just meant—"

He pushes his plate away. "Life is joyless. It's drudgery."

"But you have the means to do so much."

"I have the means to build myself a monument then have some bitch knock it down and spend my money! Are you kidding? I'm done!"

I push the bowl of soup away and eat a stale saltine cracker.

He opens a pill case, neatly marked with the days of the week. "Are those vitamins?"

"Anti-depressants."

"Oh, I see."

"You don't see. You don't see at all. You women don't see. All you see are dollar signs."

"Well, fortunately, I don't need your money or anyone else's. I have a thriving practice and a successful book."

"Another therapist. Another vagina with a Ph.d. You're all the same."

"Hey, sorry I got you on a bad night. But I'm going to grab a taxi and head home."

I open my wallet and drop two twenties on the table. He doesn't look up. He's counting out his pills and frowning.

Outside, I hurry to my car, and when I cross the Golden Gate Bridge, inhaling the fog, I feel suddenly new.

Boomer Intellectual

*E*than Krups is sixty-eight, has blond curly hair, a Ph.d in French literature, a British accent, and lazy dark eyes behind huge, red-rimmed eyeglasses. He quotes Shakespeare at the drop of a dime, brings me great books by Gertrude Stein, Fitzgerald, Hemingway, and biographies of artists I love. He also brings me obscure books by philosophers I never heard of.

He wears sandals and black socks and hideous Hawaiian shirts. He drives an old car with a stick shift. "Why buy new when the old works fine?" he says. The car stalls on the hills, and it's scary driving with Ethan.

Today, we go to an obscure sixteenth-century French concert at the museum. It's quite beautiful. The crowd consists of professorial couples, the women wearing silk shawls from India, and the men wearing natty dark jackets. A quiet, reflective crowd. A crowd of intellects, as closed as a club.

At dinner at an obscure seafood café, overlooking the ocean, over filet of sole and martinis, we discuss Fitzgerald's *The Great Gatsby*. Just talking about Gatsby makes me cry. How he yearned for Daisy, the blue light at the end of the pier, his untimely death at the end. "The unfairness of life," I sob.

Ethan pats my hand. "You remind me a bit of Gatsby. You believe in fate, in love, in that fucking blue light at the end of the pier."

"I do." I pat my eyes with a Kleenex.

"Sometimes your great love is in front of you and you don't know it."

"Like you?"

"Could be."

"You're twenty years younger."

"Gatsby didn't think about age. I'm surprised you mention age. That's so...ordinary."

Afterwards, we go back to Ethan's flat. It's really nice. A real San Francisco flat, wood-paneled walls, high molded ceilings, arched windows, and window seats stacked with pyramids of books.

He turns on his stereo. Gluck plays. We sit on a loveseat, and we kiss. The kissing is good. For a moment, I imagine Sundays in France, reading French poetry to each other, listening to Renaissance music. I'm getting turned on.

We kiss again. I place my hand there and am relieved that he has a bundle and not one of those pencil jobs.

"No," he says, pushing my hand away.

"No, what?"

"I don't do it."

"*It* what?"

"It gets me into trouble. I'm not interested in sex anymore. Let's read poetry."

So now, he reads Wordsworth, than Keats, his gorgeous voice and accent turning me on. I'm in a swoon. If it isn't one thing, then it's another, I think.

"You see, Katy? Poetry is truly sexual."

"Uh-huh."

"Orgasms are for dogs."

"I see."

"With literature you don't need sex. It's ugly. Shrill. Creepy."

"I see."

His face is scrunched up. "Sex is for the birds. It's quick, fast, nothing. You're left with nothing. Listen to these words, Katy."

He reads a poem by Plath.

I close my eyes, listening, imagining what complete love is. He's smart, sensitive to poetry, but he's fucked up. So far, there's something wrong with all these guys. What happens to their development? Are we caught between generations—women in one place and the men in another—or is it ageism all the way? But, ah, love—I imagine love comes as softly as the scent of lilacs on a summer day.

THE BOOMER HOTTIES

"George and I are getting married," Niki says.

"What?"

"Married."

"Oh, my God," we all chant. The boomer hotties and I are at having lunch at the Cliff House, overlooking the beach and the ocean and Seal Rock. Hundreds of seals lounge on the tall rocks like long, black gloves.

As Niki glowingly talks about how George surprised her on Valentine's Day with a proposal, that he can't live without her, doesn't want to live with out her, I'm thinking there is something so magical, so marvelous about boomer love. Niki is mature, emotionally and financially independent, a woman of the new generation, and George is a forward-thinking man, and they're going to partner together.

"Well, Chang and I are thinking marriage is good. Long as you stake your end of the room," Lorraine says.

"Poor Bunny would trade places with you. She's now with a new freak, who makes her wear high heels during sex, and she just had hip surgery."

"Women must stop trading up their needs, comforts, for a man. This still exists," Marcy says.

175

"Look who's talking," Sandy says angrily to Marcy. "You give your freak everything. Sold your house, moved into a house on top of a secluded mountain."

"It's beautiful there," Marcy says. "We love it."

"It's so high on the mountain that your freak face can push you off the ledge, and on one would ever know."

"And he'd have your money," Lorraine chides.

"Let's not judge. Let's be happy for Niki."

And as the girls talk at once about plans to give Niki and George a dinner, I watch the ships float under the bridge, slowly moving into new destinations.

Life is like that. There's always a new journey to take. There's always change.

THE BOOMER HOTTIES
ON THE PHONE

"**I** warned you not to see the professor again. Lorraine was right," Sandy says.

"All right, so I did."

"Was it worth it?"

"Last night, he was great. Sexy. He whispered that he loved me."

"Until today. When he had to get home to the Russian."

"Well he's done. This time it's for real. Plus, I have cystitis again. I have to take those purple pills. At Walgreen's, I stood in line and bought those friggin pills like a teenager."

"You don't need another bladder infection."

Beeep.

"I knew this would happen," Niki says. "Sandy told me—"

"Well, anyway, it's over."

"Honey, go out with others. You don't need him."

"How's George?"

"Divine."

"Has he called?"

"Five days ago."

"He's a sixty-year-old man. And he's pulling that not-calling-after-sex shit. Five days is a bad sign."

"Well, his daughter was ill and h—"

"Beeep.

"Mom! You haven't called. You haven't told me how it was with the jerk."

"Fine."

"Which means he's done. I know the tone."

"It's over."

"Till the next time," she sighs.

"Talk later."

Jesse Jankowitz

March is windy, and a gray light turns the trees silver. A lot is happening. Josh calls constantly, promising that if I go back to him, things will be different. "I'll change," he promises. But, no. I know he won't. Been there, done that. So, sadly, I told him it's best that he doesn't call again. Sometimes you just have to let things go, and I believe that the kind of sexual relationship that we had will not let us be friends. We just can't. Not that I devalue what we did have, but now when I look back, I see myself as playing a dangerous game and never having the intimacy I so desire.

The sequel *Boomer Heat Two* sold to a major publisher. Also, the film option is still alive. Who knows? You never know with Hollywood, but it's exciting, and I believe it will happen. Also, my practice is booming, and I'm working with new and interesting patients. Plus, I'm booked to perform *Boomer Heat* at the Commonwealth Club soon; this process is part of my fate, of something I don't know yet.

Sometimes I feel that time is going so fast that I won't get to do what I want to do—say what I want to say. Maybe that's the beauty of aging—as a rose bursts into bloom, then opens.

Today, it's a muggy San Francisco day. A golden light lies over the city, highlighting the hills like candlelight. It's Saturday afternoon, and I have a peaceful alone day with no plans. I love this kind of day. I'm at the organic market, picking out tomatoes. I'm going to make pasta sauce for my pasta and watch movies tonight.

"Hello, Katy."

I turn around. It's Jesse Jankowitz, the director I'd met at Starbucks months ago. I feel myself flush. "Oh, hello. Nice to see you again."

He wears a black t-shirt over cargo pants with pockets on the sides. His wavy silver hair is long in the back.

"You, too, Katy. I've been in France, making my new film. I wanted to call you, get together, but time got away."

"What's your film about?" I ask eagerly.

"Joan Mitchell. It's about her struggle as a woman and an artist."

"I love her color, music, sensuality. Everything about her paintings is unique and gorgeous. I was sad when her lover Michael Goldberg married someone else—then her long affair in Paris with Jean Paul Riopelle—"

"So you know her work?"

"I paint. I've always admired Mitchell's personal use of color, aggressive use of the paint, and her intellect—the music in her work is sensual. Anyway, I love her work," I repeat, tomatoes still in my hand.

"Sounds like you know a lot about modern art."

"I don't, but I love contemporary art. But I think all art documents life."

Silence. He looks reflective, as if lost in a thought.

"Nice tomatoes here," I say, after a long silence.

"Organic. My wife liked this market."

"The tomatoes are fresh," I say, furious with myself for feeling flustered. "I'm making shrimp pasta with mushrooms, basil—my grandmother's recipe," I add nervously. When I'm nervous, I talk fast and too much. "Anyway, do you think red peppers would be good?" I ask, hating myself for talking so much.

So then, he starts telling me how to make sauce with peppers and mushrooms, and we're both clinging to our tomatoes. After a self-conscious pause, he says, "I have an idea. What if I make the pasta, and you make the sauce? I'll bring wine and French bread."

"Oh, that sounds great. When?"

"Tonight."

"Really? Oh, that's...great."

"What time is good for you, Katy?" He grins, as if he's amused by my fluster.

"Seven. Casual."

"I have your address from your card. See you then."

"Tonight? Are you crazy?" Nanny shouts on the phone. "Why didn't you say you're busy? Now he knows you're eager."

"I am. I admire this man."

"Admire or not, you need to play hard to get. Now with the cooking pasta. Oh, my God, Mom, you have to listen to your Nanny."

"Gotta go."

The rest of the day, I clean the loft, set the small glass table with my orange plates I bought in Chinatown. They have gold birds on them. I fold the bright turquoise linen napkins. An hour left. I rush to the flower mart and buy orange tulips. I arrange them inside my violet glass vase from Venice, then light votive candles.

Casual, I'd said. Okay. I wear my new skinny jeans, open flat sandals, a comfortable black silk tunic, and long turquoise earrings.

I'm ready. Ten minutes before seven, I adjust the track lights on the paintings of women wearing red hats and see-through dresses, and play the new CD of French songs.

The doorbell rings.

PASTA AND LOVE

He carries a huge pot of pasta and a bouquet of yellow roses.

"They are beautiful, thank you," I say, arranging them into a square glass vase.

He places the beautiful pot of pasta on the marble counter then he looks around. "I like your space," he says. He moves close to a fourteen-foot painting on the wall.

"The woman in this painting is haunting. Did you paint this?"

I nod.

"The woman is hidden."

"Well, I think art is what's underneath, and sometimes the secrets show up."

I pour red wine into two glasses, and we sit on the long leather couch in front of the window. Twilight lies over the city like a long, gray coat. Foghorns blow, and the sounds of ship bells at the end of the pier mingle with the sound of the rising wind.

Easily, we talk about our work—my new book project, and about my experience with the film option—he, about the difficulties setting his film in the fifties and sixties art world. We're nibbling on Brie cheese and crackers and sipping the beautiful wine. He has the most beautiful voice, I think, careful diction, every word, as if edited.

"Everything looks delicious, Katy." He holds my chair while I sit at the table.

The pasta is sensational, and between drinking wine and eating, we talk about everything from our adult children to our tastes in art.

"I admire your dialogue," I say. "It says what's not said. It's felt."

"I imagine that is how you work when you're treating a patient?"

"The listening is very important. Listening to the silences."

He's quiet now.

"I can tell you love your work," he says. "I read *Boomer Heat*, and the case histories are insightful and interesting. Also, your paintings have a radiance about them."

We continue to talk about the process of work. He is modest, even tentative when he speaks about his films, but he's full of animated passion for its process. Also, he collects contemporary art by unknown painters. He owns a loft in New York, where he and his wife spent a great deal of time with artists and writers, and he's looking forward to filming in New York.

"Sounds marvelous," I say. "I love New York."

The music changes to a violinist playing more French songs.

Suddenly, he glances at his watch. "It's late, Katy. Thank you for having me tonight. I find you interesting. I'd like to see you again."

"I'd like that, too," I say, feeling shy. "I'll wash your pot and give it to you next time."

He kisses me lightly on the lips, a warm kiss.

After I close the door, I blow out the candles. I stand in the middle of the room, inhaling his scent, a mixture of mint and trees. I put an ice cube in the vase of yellow roses. An ice cube makes the flowers last longer.

Then I go to the phone. Sandy stays awake past midnight, watching movies. I tell her about Jesse, every detail of the evening, down to the

184

delicious pasta, the roses, how sincere he is. "He's mature, brilliant, vulnerable, and confident. He's the real thing. He acts like a real man, not some freak trying to recapture his youth."

"Honey, have you been drinking?"

"No, seriously. I mean it."

"Something sounds fishy."

"Nothing is fishy. He's fabulous."

"Did he ask to see you again?"

"He said he wanted to. I know he'll call."

"Sounds like a keeper."

"He was happily married for over fifty years. Probably still has her bed."

"Honey, if you decide he's the one—bed, schemed—you won't care. You may consider it an honor, even. Gotta go. *Casino* is on. Love that movie. Oh, I didn't tell you. Bunny Blumenthal eloped with the Iranian prince. Some prince. She had to pay for the honeymoon."

"But maybe she's happy. Everyone has their own way of finding happiness. Anyway, I'll see you at Lorraine's poetry reading next Sunday."

Beeep.

"Mom. I know it's late. Can you talk? How was your date?"

"Do you ever sleep?"

"Did he ask you out again?"

"He said he'll call."

"Same old, same old."

"He will."

"Play it cool."

"Not too cool," I say.

"Mom," she croons in a baby voice. "Get some sleep. You're too old to be obsessing over another freak at this hour."

POETRY READING

Jesse called the next morning. He invited me to the theater the next night. Anyway, it's Sunday afternoon. I'm at Lorraine's fabulous house on the tip of Chinatown. It has a red pagoda roof. Inside, it's magnificently decorated with murals of Ama, the Indian healer, along with Chinese panels of landscapes. Chinese rugs with warm colors of gold and orange and blue are strewn about the stained wood floors. The kitchen is steel, and the walls are red. The potluck lunch is marvelous. Poets carry platters of homemade salads, noodles, mushroom dishes, and Lorraine serves wine. Her just-released poetry books are piled on one table, the image of one of my floral paintings, a spray of yellow and orange flowers, as the cover.

A group of well-known poets, along with Niki, George, Sandy, Marcy, and me, sit in a circle around a large teak coffee table. The French doors open to a small courtyard, where stone fountains spurt water, and umbrella trees drape the stone benches and drag shadows along the brick floors.

Lorraine, dressed in a long, gold brocade silk Chinese jacket and gold silk flowers in her hair, announces that she's going to read and that live music will play.

A beautiful, young Chinese couple tap a large metal circle dangling from a yellow rope. It makes a deep chime sound. Then the man, about twenty, props his violin under his chin, and the girl, also about twenty, wearing red satin, props her electric guitar and begins singing the most magnificent love songs. The violinist bows to her as he plays, and the guests are swaying.

Then after applause, Lorraine reads "Old," one of her poems about growing old. She reads: *like a tree, bending to the wind.*

After the reading and more music, we drink tea and eat rice cakes. Niki, wearing an emerald satin jacket and black pants, takes me aside.

"Has he called?"

"This morning. We're going to a play tomorrow night."

"When they invite you out right away and for a Monday night, they're interested."

"Be cool," Sandy advises, joining our group.

"Look at poor Marcy. So lovely, and hanging on that drip. On her hard-earned money, he bought a six-figure electric car, only the dummy runs out of batteries on the Golden Gate Bridge, and there's no charging station. So poor Marcy had to walk across the bridge to get help, schlepping in her new Prada shoes while Mr. Freak sat in the car on his new phone. His latest performance piece is that he sits in a bucket nude, and the viewer is supposed to set the hose of water on him."

"He's nuts."

"She's nuts," Sandy snorts.

"She's not. Something works for her. She'll find her way out."

"Who knows if that'll happen," Niki says. "But we're sisters. We're here to support each other."

We join hands, and for the rest of the afternoon, we sit in the courtyard, laughing and telling each other stories.

JESSE

Since the first night Jesse and I had dinner, we've been seeing each other steadily for several weeks. We've gone to films, art openings, and simple cafes for early dinners. I've enjoyed Jesse, his intellect, and talking about our work. I feel like I imagine one feels when falling in love—this deep admiration for the person and at the same time, daydreaming about him, and wondering what sex would be like with him, watching his films over and over again, thinking about our last kiss and giggling. Talking endlessly with the girls about him, about his every smile, sigh, wondering why he doesn't call for days, the way he walks, all forward, as if hurrying, the waves in his hair tied long in the back, his deep, emotional voice.

Today, Jesse and I are having a late lunch at the Crab Shack at the end of the pier. Often, he calls after my last patient, and when he's free, we have a late lunch, and then walk for miles along the ocean, picking up shells, talking about the light in the sky. Jesse wears a Giants baseball cap, shielding his eyes from the white light facing us. We're on the terrace outside. I wear dark glasses and a long, turtleneck sweater over my leggings, as I've just come from work. The crab is delicious, and we dip the fresh crabmeat into a lemon sauce.

"Are you with someone?" I blurt, holding my hand on my forehead, as if shielding my glasses from added light, but really not wanting him to see how nervous I feel.

Jesse looks at me curiously.

"I mean with a woman?" I persist.

"Would I be spending time with you if I were?"

"Probably."

He laughs. When he laughs, he glows. "Katy, you're funny."

"Not that it's my business," I continue after a long silence. "Nor do I want to sound confrontational. It's just that—oh, now I'm all flustered."

He smiles. "After my wife died, I wasn't interested in going out with a date. Until you."

"Wow. Wowie."

"I'm very attracted to you."

"Really?"

He laughs again. "You know I am."

"I'm bonks over you. I was attracted to you the first time I met you at Starbucks. There, I said it."

He holds my hand, gently, like holding a flower. Seagulls swoop low, like gray chiffon. "This is the first time I'm being honest. Maybe I sound like an emotional moron, but with you, I don't mind being... vulnerable."

"Katy, I'm not looking for a fling or an affair. I'm looking for a deep friendship. I feel connected to you."

"Whoopee. But I'm a neurotic mess. I've never had a real close relationship."

He drinks his wine, and for a moment, we gaze at the wind blowing the waves like layers of lace.

He pauses. "Why don't you come with me to New York? We'll look at art; you'll meet many artists from Mitchell's life."

"Oh my God. I'd be a nervous wreck, wondering if I'm doing everything right. If you'd still like me. If you'd see how I look in the morning—my eyes get puffy and I have to put teabags on the bags. I'm too scared to get Botox, stuff like that, but—"

"Katy, we'll have a great time. Please say yes."

"Yes."

Later that day, I write in my case history: "You made the first move. A big move for you. Be scared. Be anxious. Those are honest emotions. Don't be like your patient George, who has to pretend all the time, who has to hide behind his Botox, and couture clothes. Isn't love at times as tentative as a lost butterfly—"

BOOMER HOTTIES

"You're not going, are you?"

"Yes."

"Mom, you've only dated the guy a few times."

"But he's not just a guy. He's special. We're both interested in art, and he's making a film about Joan Mitchell—"

Beeep.

"Hold on, Nanny."

"Tell your freaks they can wait."

"Sandy, hi. I'm on the phone with Nanny."

"Lorraine told me you're going to New York with Jesse. You go, girl."

"You think?"

"Go, honey. How long do you think we have? Don't wait. Look what happened to Holly. She holds off on the rich software designer from Silicon Valley, and he drops dead in the parking lot."

Beeep.

"Hold on."

"Katy, Marcy told me the news," Niki says exuberantly. "George and I are in Paris, but I want you to sleep in Jesse's dead wife's bed. Who cares? You're alive; she's dead, poor thing. Go for it. George says so, too."

"Not sure I'm ready for that yet," I say.

"Poor Marcy. Her freak, penniless performance artist embezzled money from her. Call her. She's devastated. Gotta go to the Eiffel Tower with my love. See you soon."

"Nanny, I'm back."

"Mom, it's cold in New York. Bring a warm coat, and I hope you don't wear those hippie H&M sweaters you wear. You're with a great guy."

"I dress as I dress."

"Dress differently, then!" she shouts. "Wear your nice pearls and a pretty suit. You're an older woman. Be elegant. Not so Taylor Swift."

"Gotta go. Love you."

NEW YORK

New York is a sizzle of noise and action. We arrive, and it's freezing, and the city is all white from frost. I love New York and recall the days Nanny went to NYU, my visits, and wonderment. Next to San Francisco, it's my favorite city in the world.

Jesse's loft is fabulous. The loft is huge, maybe six thousand square feet, with tall windows that face the New York harbor, high ceilings, and comfortable soft chairs and couches arranged for conversation.

A large diptych by Joan Mitchell, *No Birds*, takes up one wall. I'm blown away. It's so gorgeous, even more gorgeous in the flesh than the pictures of her work that I've coveted for years. The movement, the music, structure, is mind-boggling. "Oh, my God. I've never seen anything so intimate, yet splattered with emotions."

He nods. "My wife and I bought this painting in 1988. I never stop looking at it. Her structure underneath the paint is complex. The brushstrokes infinite in their passion."

For a long while, I look at this painting. "We're meeting friends for dinner," he says. "Let's freshen up."

My room is next to the master room. It is a cheerful room with long windows and a wood dresser, bathroom, and double-size bed.

"Make yourself comfortable," he says.

After I freshen up and change to my black jeans, new cashmere black sweater, boots, and long coat, I meet Jesse in the living area. He's on the phone for a while, going over his plans to shoot scenes. I decide that on some of these days I will spend time at the museums, and meet my publisher.

"Let's go," he says. "My friends will be waiting."

Outside, it's really raining now and almost eight o'clock. The city is a boom of noise—sirens, horns, and people. It's alive! We're walking along Canal Street, holding hands. Am I dreaming? Here I am in New York with this marvelous person, and I'm happy. I've never been so happy—not only with myself, but with another human being. Jesse walks fast, on his toes, as if hurrying forward, and when we talk, our breath makes white spirals.

We arrive at a small Italian café and hurry down a narrow flight of stairs into a warm, small room lit by candles. Jesse's friends sit at a long wood table, and he warmly greets them and introduces me as his friend Katy.

"You're Dr. Katy," says Eva Santos, a well-known actor. "Jesse said you have beautiful hazel eyes, and you do."

She has vivacious, violet eyes, stunning in an angular, sad face. Most of his friends are actors, cameramen, and scriptwriters. All are involved in art. They wear black pants, high boots, and possessed expressions on their faces. We drink vodka and eat sausage and anchovy pizza. It's so good, and I'm trying not to eat like a pig. Anyway, everyone is talking animatedly about the art world's insulated environment, how badly Joan Mitchell, Lee Krasner, and other great woman artists were treated.

"They were labeled woman artists," I say. "No one should be labeled anything."

"I'll drink to that," Jesse says, raising his glass.

"So you write and paint, we hear," says a thin man with a long beard. He is Jesse's top cameraman. Jesse said that he's also a very notable collector of contemporary art.

"Katy's paintings of women wearing hats are very interesting—macabre," Jesse says eagerly.

"Hats? What do the hats mean?"

"They hide under the hats. I don't like to paint faces."

"Interesting," says a very beautiful girl about thirty. Also an actor in Jesse's movie, she has the most interesting face—black, thick eyebrows like wings and deep-set green eyes, and the palest skin I'd ever seen. "Sounds like she's hiding something."

"As most women do," I say.

Another man, also a cameraman and collector, talks about his buying sprees of unknown New York art.

"I buy what's in the community," he continues. "Not this string shit that grows in museum basements or in socialites' fancy condominiums! Joan Mitchell, De Kooning, Pollack, Matisse, they painted with their souls, musicality, substance."

"The world is hard on woman artists," says the pale blonde, now enjoying the discussion. "We're supposed to be hostesses and wives. We're supposed to treat art as a hobby, while the male artist gets all the accolades."

Eva says animatedly, "Unless we make mobiles for cribs, or tiny ballerinas for glass cases, or act in roles of wayward women, we're considered useless."

"Van Gogh's ear is the art world's resurrection," said Screech Kornblum. He's a scriptwriter.

They discuss books, then Kierkegaard, arguing for the Rotation Method. The talk turns to method acting. I wonder if inside all of us is a true characterization, one that no one sees, and to act, to truly act, is to get in touch with that raw person inside of us. Anyway, it's a festive crowd, an evening of fun. Past midnight, we return to the loft.

"You must be exhausted. Jet-lagged," he says. "Get some sleep. I'm leaving at five a.m. to shoot a scene uptown. I'll leave the address where I am. I hope you come by. I'll have a chair for you to watch."

"I'm lunching with my publisher for the second edition of *Boomer Heat*. If I don't, I'll see you tomorrow night."

He hugs me and kisses me warmly.

I'm so tired, that I once I'm in bed, I slide into a dreamless sleep.

THE PUBLISHER

When I awake, Jesse is already gone. Exhausted, I'd slept until nine a.m. After I dressed, I went into the kitchen. Jesse left a sweet note with his cell phone number on it, reminding me to call if I wanted to meet him. He said he'd be working all day and that we'd meet at Nates Bar at seven o'clock, around the corner from his loft.

Coffee is made and heated. I pour coffee into a large red mug and sit by the window, watching the rain fall over New York.

After I drink my coffee and finish dressing, I call a taxi to Starlight Publishers on East Forty-Fifth Street.

Outside, I call a taxi, and when I arrive at the tall, narrow building, I hurry inside, already soaked.

My publisher/editor Jane Escher is in her late fifties, a small, austere woman with dark, wavy hair and humorless gray eyes. Her office is a cozy room with piles of manuscripts neatly arranged on a long, glass desk. Jane lights a cigarette. "Do you mind?" she asks, exhaling a stream of smoke.

"No, not at all." I cough, hold my breath against the smoke.

"I think *Boomer Heat Two* is going to do very well. Especially the case histories of women over sixty. Very timely and interesting."

"I'm glad."

"I'm going to promote the book internationally. Also, you have an audio deal."

"You mean someone is actually reading aloud these case histories?"

"Oh yes. There's a market for this. I'm going to promote your book as creative non-fiction because of the interesting way you lay out the histories. Also, you have an option, so there will be more demand."

"If the option goes."

"Most of them don't," she says, jabbing her half-smoked cigarette into the ashtray. Her nails are painted a deep blue, deceiving next to her conservative tweed suit. "I'm a fifty-six-year-old single woman," she says. "I relate to not only the case histories of aging men, but to the neuroses that's set into our country. The *age rage*, as you say."

We talk for quite a while. She orders sandwiches in, and we chat about the book—the galleys—the pub date, which will be late spring. After a while, I leave, and still snowing, I decide to walk for a while. For most of the afternoon, I walk, stopping at a cafe to have an espresso and enjoy my contentment. To record the moment.

The next few days are glorious, like in a dream. I feel like I'm in this movie, like Madison County with Francesca and Clint Eastwood. When Clint says, "This kind of certainty only comes once in a lifetime," I die. Die a thousand hearts. Is this really happening to me? Lord, thank you, I say. It's not having a man in my life; it's having this connection, this deep feeling like I've never had, one that can happen at every age. Between working, Jesse takes me to meet well-known painters in their lofts. We eat pasta and drink red wine and talk about Jesse's film. We spend hours at galleries and museums, at Joan Mitchell's lofts, restaurants, bars she frequented. We dine late at Chinese restaurants with red carpets and gold dragons on the walls. We have lunch on the sets, and I meet the actors, cameramen, producers, costume designers. It's a world in itself, an exciting world, a piece-by-piece putting together of Joan Mitchell's world.

Tonight we're at a small dive with a few of Jesse's colleagues. He's had a long, grueling day. The talk turns to Joan Mitchell and her place with the Abstract Expressionists.

"Woman artists still are not treated with the respect they deserve," argues Jesse. "All the public knows is Studio 54 and Andy Warhol's pop flowers."

"Rock stars are paid," says Amanda, a well-known African dancer. "Why not visual artists?" Cuban music. Jesse plays the bongos, his eyes closed, his graceful hands pounding the drums to the rhythm.

When we leave the club, it's past midnight. A sudden storm covers the streets in thick, white ice. Huddling in each other's arms, we walk back to Jesse's loft, not far from the club, laughing and sliding on the ice.

Back at the loft, Jesse and I drink a decaf espresso, rehashing the evening. He shows me his storyboard for scenes the next day.

"Tomorrow, I'm leaving at noon, Jesse. I have to get back to my patients—work."

"Stay. Stay another few days. We're having a wonderful time, don't you think?"

I nod.

"Maybe that's why you want to go home? Because you are?"

He snaps off the lights. I follow him into his bedroom. Shivering from the sudden cold, I undress, and before he's even undressed, I go into his bed. It doesn't matter that photographs of Jesse and his wife hang all over the room, or that the lovely quilt on the bed is one she'd made, he said proudly. I admire his devotion. His respect for her. Nothing matters but now, but this lovely time together.

After we make love, silent, warm love, we lie in each other's arms, holding hands and watching the snowflakes. It was great. He was loving, and sexy at the same time.

"I loved having you with me tonight. You are adorable, bright, sexy," he says, kissing my mouth.

"Sounds like my eulogy."

He laughs, throwing back his head. "You eagerly embrace me, yet you hold back. When I want to go to the next step, you pull away."

"I need time."

"Time for what, Katy? This is our time. It's now. Don't rush home tomorrow. Stay."

"I have to go to Los Angeles for my movie then I have new patients. Maybe another time. Don't you think? Do you hear me? Let's treasure our time together. Know that we're bound forever. Our moments are so lovely. Let's not spoil them with expectations. Time. Do you hear me?"

Jesse is sleeping. Snoring, actually. His arms are around my waist. When he snores he exhales a thin slow whistle. The storm has stopped. For a long time, I listen to the silence of the dawn, knowing that I must return home. I have work—the movie, patients, and I love my life. Or is that the real reason? Am I getting back into my wanting to be alone, and have a relationship on my terms? Or do I think he'll end up like the rest? Oh well, don't' analyze it to death.

I'll figure it out. I watch the snow, thinking I love the silence of the snow, and then I close my eyes and slip into sleep. And I'm dancing the tango, still klutzy but this time I know I'm dancing with Jesse. I see his face.

Then I run along the side of the ocean, my bare feet slapping the wet sand, my arms out to balance myself so I won't fall, and the sky is low, and a huge rainbow shimmers in front of me, and I'm about to run through it…

END

Acknowledgments

I want to thank all the people who have helped me, and there isn't room to name all of them. With each book, there's a journey and help. You know who you are:

To my brother Robbie and gratitude for his encouragement. Special gratitude to Matthew Carlini for his consistent help and expertise and helping me polish this book. My thanks to Deborah Greenspan at Llumina Press for her professionalism; Also, special thanks to Shari Reimann, for her excellent work. Barry Miller and David Weiner for their PR and love; Gerry Astrove and Donald Alex for their unconditional support; Barbara Brenner for her art and friendship; Marlene Levinson for her lifelong friendship and support; Judith Cohen for her laughter, decorating, and lifelong friendship; John Milner for his support and for always letting me speak my truth at the SF Commonwealth Club. Always, thanks to Tara Cortez for going beyond friendship and for her expert promotion and marketing skills; Alex Ari, for his publicity and friendship; Liz Harris, my editor at the Jweekly; Riki Rafner, for having me on her shows and fun; Beatrice Livitsky for taking me in when I was stuck and for her delightful company; Ramani Wright for her charm and for India and Dan Max for friendship. Thanks and love to my smart, loving cousins, Donald Krauss, Linda Diller, Penny Berman; always Mira Paskinov for her intellect and books; Mia Stageberg, Kathy Lerner, and David, BFFs forever; Patty Axelrod for always being there. Jerry Asttove, Donald Alex, always love. Always gratitude and love to Bradley, Bessey, Frank, and Gabriel; Richard Ayoub always.

Special thanks to Debra Martin Chase for caring. For SFSU/OLLI - Andrea Rouah, Marsha Michaels, Sue Woods, Cathy Fiorella, for their talents, Francie Covington for her dancing shoes, Barbara Blumenfeld for all the rides, Vivian Zielin always, and Sandra Halliday for letting me teach at OLLI. Patti Ross, always, and Norma Kaufman for her dedicated friendship. Dr. Bill Smith, Dr. Donnelly, a great dentist; Diane Baker for her beauty, acting, and kindness; Janet Sipos, my favorite redhead; Tasia Melvin for her unconditional support; Susan Savage always. Florence Osterman and in memory of Horace Osterman and family, Thanks to Rose Wang for always being there and for beautiful hair styling; Aparna Sain for friendship and India-Diane Rosenberg, always, and her son, David Rosenberg for his courage; Lily Marshall Fricker for your smarts and beauty. Always, Lori Marshall for your friendship; Dr. Janine Canan, a favorite poet; Andrea Rouah for your faith and for SFSU; Sandra Halliday for letting me teach at Olli; Barbara Repa, for her artistic spirit. Eileen Williams for listening, and smarts; Billy Winters for his photography; special thanks to all the kids at SF Polk/Vallejo Starbucks; Patti Felker and Chris Abramson for their legal expertise, Ned Cogswell, and Jordan Foland, for their writing and taking risk in helping me-- and everyone I didn't mention - Thank you